# A Da

By J D Wallace

Drin who always reminds me how far I have come and how far I still need to travel.

**Published 2017 by JD Wallace**

**Through Libertate Publishing**

Books by J D Wallace


The Boarder

The Dragon That Guards the Center

A Lion at the Gate of The Temple

Cat from the Second World

Journey of the Four Ancients

A Darker Will to Live


Jade

A Lucky Star


Rhyming Words with Carolyn Chau

*Figure 1 Drakson home*

# A Business Meeting

*Three years ago*

The office seemed small for a CEO. The nature of the company might have afforded an executive much larger accommodations. It was nearly twenty feet on each side. For a mid-level manager, it might be considered large but Jamas was here to see the top brass.

The room was undecorated. A standard office desk had nothing on it. The walls contained no art or family photos. A large window looked over an area of Tokyo dominated by tall towers. The room seemed unfriendly and enclosed.

Two doors offered access to the room. The one she'd entered allowed access through a reception area back to the main hall. The other was set in the right-hand wall. Both were exactly centered.

There were only three chairs in the room. The one behind the desk was a standard armless desk chair that could be purchased anywhere. The other two where tan leather armchairs which would have been perfect in a low rent apartment lobby. The tall woman sat uncomfortably in one of the leather armchairs.

Jamas was an American. Her dark skin and lithe frame gave her an athletic and mysterious caste. Her clothing supported the image.

She wore a three-piece suite tailored for a woman. The shirt was white but otherwise the entire ensemble was black. The vest was satin and embroidered with single thread characters from a dozen Asian languages. Along the seams of every part of the outfit, more single thread characters from a dozen Asian languages exposed a style that seemed to express either an unexplainable affinity for linguistics, or a determined academic.

The pants were close cut and functional. The jacket seemed to be slightly shorter than normal. Gussets which allowed a large range of movement were sewn in strategic locations.

Her black pumps seemed chosen for functionality over appearance. Though made to resemble heels with a pointing toe, the soft rubber sole and flexible material allowed her full use of her considerable athletic ability.

She waited patiently. Her moment would come. She had set the appointment knowing that the rules were strict. The corporation had a compliment of documents she'd signed before being allowed to meet with its leader.

No recording devices were allowed. No pictures could be taken. She would not even be able to retain her cell phone during the interview. A strict policy of what type of questions she could ask were presented. This included several pages of off limits topics.

Still, she hated to wait. Though disciplined, patience was not among her virtues. Still, she waited.

The door at the right of the office opened. A lean Asian man stepped in and smiled before dropping his gaze back to a folder he carried. As he walked to the chair and sat, he paged through and seemed to make mental notes of the contents. For a moment, he sat in silent contemplation. Then, in an almost violent movement, he tossed the folder onto the desk and looked up at his guest.

"I thank you for your patience. I am Orochi," he said in a staggered English. "What can I do for you?"

Jamas was aware that the man had probably used the folder as a tactic to show he was important and busy. He might be trying to show that he offered her time only reluctantly. His manner of questioning seemed to reinforce the theory.

"I am here to learn about the way your company operates," she said in perfect Japanese. "I've been told it is a model of efficiency. For instance, you have a very effective direct marketing method which allows you to minimize maintaining stock on hand. I understand that your motto is factory direct to consumer?" She asked already knowing the answer.

Whatever his answer, she was not really here to learn from him. Her purpose was less tangible. Rumors had surfaced of an evil creature haunting the night clubs of the Shibuya district. One of those rumors linked the CEO to several deaths in the area. Though she was dubious, it was the only verifiable lead she'd had so far. So, she was here to see for herself if the man had any connection to corruption.

The treads of satin which made up characters along the lapel of her shirt were actually spells. These, like all the others, had been woven in as a way of storing the energy and recording the desired effect of the spell. A simple word or motion was all that was needed to activate them. The spell she activated should allow her to see the traces of vital energy that a creature of corruption radiated.

He right hand made a swift circular motion followed by a flick that sent the spell unobtrusively toward Orochi. To her surprise, he began to glow with a pale but deep red radiance. She'd expected to see a more traditional glittery effect.

What this told her was that her theory was incorrect. This man was not infected with corruption as used by the ancient enemy. Instead he carried a more earthly evil. She would need to do a great deal of research to figure out what the man sitting across from her really was.

The dark red aura was her only clue. Whatever he was, she still felt it her obligation to stop him from spreading his particular brand of evil. Corporate CEO or not, her duty was clear.

Orochi had finished explaining the basic premise of the company. Each order was directed to the factory where the awaiting components were assembled and shipped to the customer. Since many of the options were software related as opposed to hardware, the assembly time could be reduced to only a few hours of configuring the proper device drivers and installing the requisite programs. True, a person with reasonable knowledge of computers could add drivers and software that might unlock higher priced features. The overall cost of alternate configurations of the hardware outweighed the benefit. So, it became a more reasonable approach to simply ignore the possibility and maintain the simpler approach.

Orochi continued to espouse the idea that all the primary software for the device was proprietorial and could only be purchased from his company. Many of the specialty drivers were embedded into the device itself making it somewhat harder to upgrade without flashing the built-in BIOS with new instructions.

Though a small group of competent hackers had already managed to create customizations, availability was still limited, and, should a customer use one of these unofficial hacks, their warranty would be voided and no further updates to the device could be performed until it was returned to factory condition.

Jamas continued to wonder about the man she sat across from. He was a competent businessman with a large potential for success. Already his wealth was measured in the billions of US dollars. Could he actually be the thing she thought he was? Was it possible that the spell she'd used might be wrong? No. He was evil. She felt it in her soul. She could sense the darkness which radiated from him. There was an aura of death surrounding him.

After a half hour of discussion, Jamas was escorted out to the waiting area and given a sample of the hand-held microcomputer developed by Orochi's company. During her interview, it had been personalized and the model was the one with the highest price point offered by the company. The logo was a stylized snake wrapped around a forearm. The snake's head rested in the palm of the hand.

The nature of corruption is that it consumes the good within a person. Over the course of the so-called infection, a mind becomes susceptible to a sort of possession. For everyone, the effect might be slightly different and, in some cases, it is more of a symbiotic relationship.

Across from Jamas sat a man who seemed to have all the hallmarks of corruption but none of the normal detectible signs.  She felt a very palpable evil from him.  That by itself seemed to indicate she should act against him if she could.

How to proceed was less obvious.  A direct confrontation seemed out of the question for now.  Though she sensed the darkness in him, she was not sure if he was the target of her recent investigations.  That was one of the things she wanted to learn from this visit.  The answer she'd received was less than affirmative and yet still she knew he had an evil aura which could indicate he was in fact the one she searched for.

A subtle plan began to form in her mind.  If she could cut him off from his support system here at the corporation, maybe he would act rashly.  She might get him to give away his hand.

One thing seemed certain, she would want to follow him and discover as much as she could before attempting anything.  Research and patience was called for.  In her heart, she was less than patient.

# Quick Thinking

*Now*

The night sky was filled with the heavy round coin of the full moon. Stars seemed to lose their brilliance next to its pale grey illumination. A halo seemed to enhance the feeling of omnipotence radiating against the darkness.

A lone, darker shadow moved between the long shadows cast by the sparse forest. Here in the trees he could move quickly. The open field ahead would offer little cover.

A tall wall of rough stone formed the boundary between the woods and the well-tended grass which formed an interruption to the wilds that surrounded the estate. As the shadow slipped into the darkness at the base of the wall, the faint sound of metal slipping against cloth could be heard.

The man hopped up and caught the edge of a stone above. This was only a foot from the top but offered excellent purchase for his lithe frame. With a quick jerk, he pulled himself up to the top of the wall and hung in a chin-up. His grey eyes scanned the area for any sign of opposition.

Once he was sure that there was no one within the immediate area, he pulled himself slowly to the top of the wall and lay down on the two foot wide parapet. He slipped the knife from its sheath at his shoulder which repeated the soft sound.

He rolled off onto the grass below, landing in a crouch. The shadows here were smaller and he could barely fit into their comfortable safety.

The man wore a dark grey utility suit with several pockets at strategic locations on the arms and thighs. A black web belt carried the barest of tactical gear. The knife in his hand and the small pistol in a flap top holster were his only weapons.

Several pouches contained other needed tools such as flashlights and survival gear.

The house across from him was large. From the briefing, he knew that the nearly ten thousand square feet structure would be a particular challenge to infiltrate. Much of the main area was formed as an open floor plan. Though modern, it provided little cover from which to conduct his reconnoiter.

To the right of the main area, the kitchen and garages opened onto a patio with an Olympic sized pool. To the left were six bedroom suites each with their own bath and a large living area.

A round drive circled the house. Though unpaved, it created the best chance of discovery. He'd decided to cross near the garages hoping there would be less chance of being spotted by one of the potential guests. Though the early morning hour would probably see most of the guests sleeping, he knew that even one could raise the alarm and ruin his mission.

Maria had asked him to check into the place after having come into possession of information related to the previous owner. There was some indication that an organized secret group might be attempting to develop a method of either reopening the now dormant gates or find alternative methods of crossing the barriers of space-time.

Nick had heard it might be possible. The metal disk created by Maria's brother Zach had seemed to allow the group to come home from the second world without actually navigating the rift. The ramifications of another way to cross the vast distances between worlds were too many to count. Maria hoped to keep this potential ability from falling into the wrong hands. Thus, Nick's raid.

Slowly, he crawled from the shadow of the wall. On his belly, he pulled himself along in almost imperceptible movements. Even though the distance was only a few dozen yards, he took nearly a half hour to cross all the way to the circular drive.

Again he waited, searching into the darkness for any sign of the guards he felt must be there. A tall man walked from the shadow of the garage. He carried a tactical rifle in a nonchalant way. Although well armed, he was obviously not well trained.

Nick waited for him to turn the corner and begin to walk away before he silently leapt to his feet and ran at a full clip toward him. The guard never heard the soft rapid steps of his death swooping in from behind.

Nick plunged his blade quickly into the side of the guard's neck and slipped into the shadow before the man fell to the ground. Leaning forward from his concealment, Nick griped the boot of the dead guard and pulled him slowly into the shadows.

Nick checked him for anything useful. The pat down revealed an ID, a pack of Russian cigarettes, a ring of keys, and only two magazines for the rifle he carried.

The keys he slipped into a pocket. Then, Nick ripped the front from the cigarette pack and rose slowly. A door flanked the garages to one side. Though a light was shining above, no one was around to see as Nick slipped through the door and into the building beyond. Three large roll up doors stood on one end of the bay. The other end offered a large workshop and a passage that would lead to the kitchen.

With no one evident, he crossed to the portal and checked for any sign of detection. He could see a camera pointed down the short passage. Anyone watching a monitor on the other end would have seen Nick step boldly into view and stride calmly down the hall to the door.  Once there, he simply opened it and walked through.

He was counting on being bold.  He wanted to seem as though he belonged in the compound.  Once inside he might fool a possible enemy into thinking he was simply part of the normal compliment of people.

Slowly he moved along the wall toward the one door which led to the interior of the garage.  A light above the door was flanked by a camera which indicated it was on by the red LED glowing steadily to the right of the lens.

By staying close to the wall, he was out of the field of view of the camera but if he opened the door, the swing of it would probably be picked up.  Though someone looking at a monitor would not see him, they would see that the door had opened.

He'd planned for this.  From a pocket, he pulled out his phone which had a relatively high resolution camera, and a small black rectangular device that had a paper tab sticking from one of the ends.  He focused the camera of the phone away from the building into the yard.  Raising his hands to a position roughly equal to the level of the camera, he took a picture.  He hoped the snapshot would give him the needed view.

He plugged the phone into a cable suspended from the other device and tabbed through to the new picture.

Once selected, a print of the photo slowly slid from the portable printer.

He replaced the devices and withdrew a small rough wire frame that seemed made from a coat hanger. He bent the long tail end of it to roughly perpendicular to the frame and using a square of tape, secured it to the frame. With another bit of tape, he fastened the assembly quickly to the top of the camera directly in front of the lens.

He hoped he'd placed it quickly enough that no one would detect the movement. He also hoped that the camera was framed closely enough on the picture for it to pass inspection for at least a short time.

The door was not locked. He slipped into the garage and moved quickly to one side of the door in an attempt to stay in whatever shadows the space might offer. There was a small vertical shadow cast by the heavy web flange structure that made up the framing in the garage. The garage was four cars wide and three deep though only seven cars currently stood waiting.

Nick moved from car to car. He stayed low and before each move he observed as much of the entire room as he could. The camera near the door which led to the kitchen slowly panned across the garage. He timed his advance to coincide with it so as not to be detected.

So far no alarm had been raised so he hoped he had not been detected yet. It was possible that he had been and the defenders might be preparing a trap of some kind.

He decided to continue with the mission. The rewards well outweighed the risk. If he managed to succeed, the group would have another insight into the enemy they'd recently discovered.

Finally, he stepped along-side the door. Again, he was in the camera's blind spot. After repeating the procedure with his camera and printer, he proceeded into the hallway leading to the interior of the home.

No lights were on inside the house. He could see past the long entry and into the kitchen only after several seconds of waiting for his eyes to adjust. Once he was ready, he moved slowly down the hall.

A small red LED ahead told him there was a camera or other electronic detection device ahead. He slipped to the opposite wall, trying to stay hidden in the darker shadow there. Once he reached the opposite end of the hall, he could see that the kitchen was a large professional style affair. The red LED was coming from some of the kitchen equipment.

Again he moved slowly. As he crossed the large room, he searched for any sign of detection. The house was still silent and no sound could be heard. A double door stood opposite of him. Vertical windows allowed visual access from one side to the other. Ostensibly this was to diminish the chance of an accident during a meal. The service staff could detect another person on the other side of the portal by looking through the windows.

The window gave Nick a chance to spy on the other room without giving away his presence. He waited there, looking from one side to the other till he was assured that the next room was empty. He also ascertained his ultimate destination. An office across from the main entrance was just to his left.

The entire front of the office was glazed. Only dark wood mullions which ran from floor to ceiling broke Nick's view of the thing he had come for.

On the large lacquered Asian desk stood a round metal object. Light seemed to reflect in troubling patters from its burnished surface. The shape reminded Nick that it was a human skull encased in brushed steel.

He crossed to the office and was relieved to find the door unlocked. Once inside he drew from a pocket a black velvet bag with a leather drawstring. Nick had been warned not to touch the skull.

He looked at it briefly, making sure that it was the thing he wanted. Though completely plated in steel, the details of the skull were not diminished. Each crack and line was in evidence. Along each of them, long lines of very fine glyphs formed the complex spells which bound incredible power to the object.

Without touching it, he dropped the sack over it and tilted the skull up. Then he drew the string tight and headed back the way he'd come. As he left the office, he pulled the drawstring out and slipped each arm through the loops, creating a makeshift backpack.

Next he crossed the kitchen and as he did so, he felt a slight twitch which he'd come to associate with danger. Though not physical in any way, the feeling had often saved him from unseen dangers. He'd come to think of it as a sort of intuition.


He slowed his movements as he opened the door leading into the garage. After looking slowly from one end of the garage to the other he stepped through and slid to the side of the door hugging the wall.

He quickly removed the photo and ring from the camera and waited for the camera to swing away before darting crossing to the nearest car. He looked up at the camera and counted. Once the camera had swung away again, he moved to his next designated cover. Finally, he was near the door. The car he was next to was a large SUV. This allowed him to stand while looking through the tinted windows to check the swing of the camera. Just as he was about to move, the door next to him opened.

Nick stepped behind the swing of the door and waited for it to close before moving against whatever target might present itself.

Four men filed in and spread out across the room. Nick tried to move quickly to the door as it swung closed, but the closest man saw him and leveled his rifle.

Nick was only about a yard from the man, which gave him ample reach to slip to the left of him. This put the man between Nick and the other three.

Nick's hands came up simultaneously and gripped the rifle just behind the flash suppressor. With a jerk to his right, the rifle was off target when it fired.

Nick brought up his guard and lifted the barrel of the rifle while twisting quickly. Nick pulled the rifle free of his enemy's hands. With a motion that seemed like a Queen Anne solute he knelt and brought the weapon up into firing position.

A quick squeeze dropped the first opponent and another leveled the next before the others could react.

Nick moved quickly to the rear of the vehicle and brought the weapon to a ready position. He stayed below the line of sight through the windows of the vehicle. He could hear the heavy footfalls of his adversaries as they advanced. Quickly he stood and fired a burst at the first target. Before he ascertained the effectiveness of the shot, he dropped again and moved quickly toward the large double door which made up the end of the car bay.

Again, he stopped and waited for any sound of the final target. This time he could hear only faint soft taps as though one remaining person was doing his best to minimize the sound he was making. Though it seemed to be coming from near the SUV he had just quitted, Nick wanted to be certain before he exposed himself again.

With all the shooting, he was sure the alarm had been raised. Speed was more important than stealth now.

Nick raced the last few yards to the garage door and with his left hand, ripped upward at the release which would disengage the door from the opening system. He spun in place as he pulled the door open and looked for the final enemy. Standing about ten feet away, a tall startled man seemed to be motionless. Nick avoided killing him by the simple expedience of running away. He'd crossed the open ground and scrambled over the wall before chase had been given.

His heavy bounty bounced against his back, reminding him that one day he might be nothing more than a skull in a bag.

# Tracking Death

*3 years ago*

Jamas returned to her hotel.  All the while she thought over the conversation she'd had and the effects of the spell she cast.  While her mandate was simply to discover and deal with corruption in the world, she felt that this danger was enough to prompt her to action.  The meaning of the red halo around Oroshi was still a mystery.  Perhaps Zach would know.

She called the house in New England after dinner.  Though late in the day in Tokyo, her home was in the early hours of the morning.  She was aware of Zach's normal schedule and knew he'd already be awake and studying in the library.  She was rewarded with his familiar scratchy voice.

"Hi, Sis," he replied after hearing her voice.  "What can I do for you?"

"I ran across something and I'm not sure what it is.  I thought you might be able to help me," she was always quick to the point.  Though her affection for the family was without doubt, she rarely showed anything more than a sort of impatience when dealing with her more academic siblings.  "I used the spell which ID's corruption.  What I got was a sort of red glow.  It seemed like a radiation of dark purpose.  I don't know if I can describe it better than that."

"The spell you used was meant to do more than simply show you corruption. When I designed it, I wanted it to express the real content of the person on whom it was cast. For instance, if you cast it on one of us you might see a pale colored light emanating from the person. The color of the light is something like a reflection of electrical coronal discharges that are captured using Kirlian photography. Though there is much speculation about the technique itself, I purposed the spell so that it would reflect the color most closely related to the person's personality. Red might mean that the person is simply very violent in nature. Normally, though, the effect is very slight. I tuned it to specifically radiate the glitter effect from a corrupted creature. If you managed to see a very well expressed corona from a person then the feature of the personality that it comes from is very, very strong," Zach informed her. "If you were to use it on me, the color blue would be there but you might not be able to make it out in normal daylight. It would only be really visible in the darkness."

"What does that mean?" She asked knowing his answer would probably be long and boring.

"I don't know," he said. "It might mean that the subject is so bound in his violence that the force of his emotion shows. The halo of each of us is a sort of field of force that allows us to interact with the world on a deeper level. Through this we can draw energy from the world to create our spells and so on. We could also become

27

more aware of things around us by tuning into the power field and using it to sense the world in ways we are otherwise unable to. Maybe this person has somehow developed that ability. I have the theory that the interaction between these fields is somehow related to corruption. But it is only a theory."

"Thanks. I think that helps," she responded. "Tell everyone hello for me."

"I will, by the way Maria is coming home. She just sent word from Asia. Something happened there and she wanted to tell father. Aunt Doris is with her."

"I'll come home as soon as I figure out what is going on here," Jamas informed him.

Maria had been off on a series of excavations with their aunt. If there was some new information she possessed, it would be interesting for her to hear. The fact that she was coming home instead of returning to her university studies meant that whatever she'd learned was important.

Jamas put that aside for the moment and decided to follow the only real lead she'd had. Various nightclubs seemed to be the last known location of the victims. She might simply stake out one of them for several nights and see what happened. If Oroshi showed up and there was a death, she would have her answer. If she could prevent a death by simply being there she would surely have to try.  After looking over the list of potential places, she selected one that had not been "hit" in several months.

Generally, she had the concern that the spells she constructed against corruption might not have an effect. Normally a spell would only work against the corruption in a creature.  She decided to run a few experiments to see if she could build a spell that effected the aura created by a person.  If she could do that, spell effects might be extended to influence humans and other life in general.

Her knowledge of spell making came from her family. Her father had given her the general overview of the skill.  The family retainer had taught her the core of her skills.  It was her mother that had offered the best insight into spell creation.

Spells are very much like martial arts techniques.  The basic movements are in and of themselves effective but do not actually express the full potential of any given spell.  For instance, you might punch a person and hit them hard.  But a combination of blocking and punching allow movement and counter effect.  Power for any given technique is generated by technical competence and emotional energy.

When several techniques are put together in a specific order, the spell can be made to have a series of complex effects which are difficult to defend against.

One of Jamas's favorite martial styles built technique based on three aspects. These are intent, skill, and focus.

Intent is what powers the spell. An intention of harm against the enemy, or to defend against an attack is drawn from the emotions of aggression and fear.

Skill is both the construction and the ability to perform the technique. Rehearsing each movement and phrase till it becomes a natural and intuitive reflex is important to every spell.

Finally, deep focus is required to draw the power through a completed intent and channel it into the skill. Focus is not as many people think. It should not be a deep breath-holding grunting sort of thing. Focus comes from a clam mind infused with intent and ordered by skill.

As Jamas prepared to test her theory about spells, she wondered how her family would react if her theory was proven to be true. Her first act would be to record it in the journals and talk to her father about the potential. If he thought it appropriate, she'd then instruct her siblings on the potential.

She began the experiment by casting the spell that allowed her to see the red glow in Oroshi. She directed it at herself. She made out a faint purple radiation of light. Small fingers of electrical energy shifted and flashed around the backdrop of her hand. She then set out to construct a spell to enhance the glow.

Spell construction is sometimes a tedious business. Like anything, the more effort you put in, the better the results. For now, Jamas was more interested in testing effect so the spells she built were simple ones that had very limited power and next to no effect.

Her first spell took only a few minutes to build. Once cast, she felt a rush of power through her hand. A flash of a dozen lines of lightning extended from her hand in a playful symphony of light. She could feel the objects around her as her now extended halo played along them.

The effect was unexpected and the rush caused her to feel somewhat lightheaded. With a little concentration, she found she could focus the lightning which flashed from her hand. With it she could feel and see things which she had been unaware of before. She felt a connection to the hotel room. She found that she could feel what had occurred here in the recent past. Her spell had given her a sort of psychokinetic sight.

She let the effect of the spell fall away.

An elation ran through her as she realized what her discovery might mean. It might be possible to create real powerful magic which could affect the real world in ways none of her family had imagined.

With that, she began to construct a series of spells which might be useful against any threat. Defense and attack were her primary focus.

The first few spells were shields of a variety of types. One would simply protect her against physical harm. The next was designed to reject any corruptive influence that she might be exposed to. Others offered protection against other challenges she might face.

For attack spells, she decided on one that would cause searing pain, another to break bones, and finally one that would expel corruption from a host. Though she knew that her adversary was not a creature of corruption, she wanted to have that one available anyway.

She then also add several detection and obfuscation spells. Because of the new type of creature, she widened the general detection spell that Zach had taught her to include more information gathering. She enhanced it with something she hoped would let her see the enemy's level of energy. If she could catch it at its weakest, she would have a better chance against it. She built another spell that she hoped would act as a kind of disguise. The intent was to prevent Oroshi from recognizing her until she acted against him. Finally, she created a spell which might be used as a sort of homing beacon.

Once completed, she sewed them into the fabric of her shirt with long black threads. As she made each stitch, she concentrated on the function of the spell and chanted the empowering components. At each apex, a knot of thread bound the spell into the material. Loose threads connecting between the knots formed the characters which made up long lines. These constituted sentences in the spell describing each effect she desired.

When a spell is woven into a garment, it imbues the wearer with a shield of energy which can be both passive and active.

Some of the spells she'd added to the already complex embroidery were meant to act as mental mazes for corruption. The mind of a creature would be drawn into the maze and trapped by the writing.

Most of the spells would simply disappear from her clothing when they were used. Each line of thread was good for one activation. It was the power she'd invested in each that allowed them to remain. Once used, the power would unwind the thread and release the desired effect.

As she set down the needle and thread, she looked at the clock. The hour was late and she'd missed her chance to act for the night. Tomorrow she would begin her stake out of the clubs. Though excited by all she'd learned she was exhausted. Creating spells took lots of energy and focus. After a quick shower, she slipped into bed and was dreaming in only a few moments.

Her dreams were of otherworldly foes. She battled against the dark shadows of her own thoughts through the night. One opponent after another faced her wrath. Each fell quickly.

Soon she realized the forms she was fighting against were familiar. Each thing seemed to be taking a feminine and powerful shape. As she fought on through the night, she found that she was fighting herself. Over and again she won. Over and again she faced her deepest most self. She fought her fear. She battled her anger. She raged against her impatience. She struggled against her arrogance.

She realized as she awoke, she had always been fighting her own demons. Knowing her dream to be a sign of truth, she meditated on the nature of her character.

It was true she was all the things she seemed to struggle against. But in all of that she understood the duality of her own nature. As each of those attributes was owned and admitted, she would continue to keep them in check. Her very own yin and yang. The circle never stops. In each there is light and dark. In darkness there is light, and in light there is darkness.

She knew she could not be true to herself without understanding both were part of her nature. The trick was to act for good even though evil was part of your personality. The struggle went on.

# The Nature of the Darkness

*3 years ago*

What is it that makes a person evil? Is it the things they have seen, the life they have lived, and the experiences they have gone through? Perhaps evil is not something that can be quantified or accessed. Perhaps it is a simple action and the resultant consequence. In the case of Oroshi, who stood in the darkest corner of the bar, it was something he'd chosen. When faced with death and oblivion or life feeding on the death of others, he chose to live. But the truth was, he'd died when the choice was made. Though he continued to exist, he was no longer among the living.

He'd hunted here before. Though it had been nearly a decade, the place changed only a little. A recent redecoration was little more than a fresh coat of paint in a similar color. Even the patrons seemed the same. Their clothing may have changed but the oblivious unconcern they showed for their eventual fate was a timeless reminder that the living were nothing more than cattle to the dark forces.

He watched, waiting for the chance to strike. The method he'd used was honed by nearly two hundred years of practice. One of the people in the room would provide him with the nourishment he needed to survive another few weeks.

He could feel the life he'd consumed recently slowly ebbing within him.  Though it hadn't been very long, the woman he'd consumed had been weak and full of impurities.  She had been an addict and her life force was weak.  It had been his best chance then so he'd taken the easy prey.  Now only a week later, he needed more.

His eyes seemed yellowed with age and the lines on his face indicated a man in late middle years.  Though full and thick, his hair also bore the greying of age mixed with his natural black.

This time he wanted someone strong and full of life.  A young and vibrant life that could sustain him for the crossing.  The right one might provide a month or more of life.  That would be enough.  It had to be enough.

He watched the door, waiting for someone that fit his requirements.  So far there were only three possibilities.  Each he'd looked over and dismissed as a secondary target should what he wanted not become available.

One woman was tall and lean and had dark European features.  For Tokyo, this was not unusual.  Often young Europeans came to the notorious club for the adventure offered.  She seemed strong and able and perhaps a little dangerous.  It might be exciting to taste the flesh of someone so powerful.  She moved like a predator, though.  Perhaps the danger she offered was real.  He had no intention of getting hurt or worse by making an unwise decision.

The others were both young Asian men. They had come in together and were obviously romantically attached to each other. They'd caressed and fondled each other most of the night. Often, they ignored their surroundings and engaged in long passionate kisses. He might not be able to separate them and that could make it dangerous.

He had the ability to calm the mind of a victim. He could force them to trust him. This would only work on one person at a time and only on someone who he could get to meet his eyes during a conversation. This required a certain amount of confidence and was at the same time the danger. He could never get a victim to do something they would not otherwise do. Finding a lone, strong, yet not too confident, person was always both a risk and a difficult thing to do.

He'd almost decided on splitting up the two men when a lone dark-haired Asian woman strolled into the club. She had more makeup on than he preferred, but he was not interested in her for romance. She was wearing a revealing short black dress with a dark purple lace at the hem and along the low-cut front. The ornate accessory accented her breasts by creating a larger upward curve. This was juxtaposed by the very narrow waist of the outfit. Her figure was barely contained. A small black sequined clutch, lacey stockings and black strapless high heels competed the image of a woman looking for a night of passion.

He waited only long enough for her to order a drink at the bar before he slowly circled the room. She had taken a seat near the end of the bar. She was not looking around, which indicated she was either alone or knew that the person she was to meet had not arrived yet. Slowly he progressed till he was a few stools down from her.

A strange change came over him as he took the last few steps toward her. His face seemed to soften and the lines disappeared. The color of his hair went from a salt and pepper to jet black. His chest swelled and the appearance of youth replaced his middle-aged features. The eyes became dark orbs within clear white. In those seconds, he seemed to rejoin the ranks of the youth that normally patronized the club.

As he loomed over her she turned. Their eyes locked for a moment. At first she was surprised and slightly offended at his abrupt approach. As the gaze held, she slowly softened till a rapport between the victim and the hunter was achieved. He knew he could ask of her anything. She knew she would do as he bid.

He reached his hand toward her and she accepted. As she stood, he set her half-finished drink on the bar, and she followed as he led her to the rear of the club where a double glass door exited to the parking garage beyond.

The flashing lights and loud music seemed to accentuate each step. Her mind wandered in a musical fantasy of what the man might offer. His deep dark eyes had seemed to promise both passion and pleasure as she'd never known. Willingly, she followed as he walked her to her death.

A shadow moved behind them. The dark tall woman who stood near the entrance quickly leapt into action. Though she was not far behind, the crowd created a barrier of moving bodies that blocked even the quick reflexes of the highly skilled woman in black.

Her clothing seemed to shine in the flashing light as though thousands of thin threads composed a symphony of writing along the seams of the pants and shirt.

The cut of the clothing was more like that of an athlete. The close-fitting leggings and loose shirt gave her complete freedom of movement. Her shoes were black with tan low cut rubber soles. Her long black hair was tied neatly into a braid which flowed like a living extension as she dove into the press of bodies that blocked her way to the man she'd been searching for.

A flash of light radiated from her arm as she uttered the single word that activated one of the lines of text along the outer seam along her sleeve. With a flick, she sent the barrier spell toward the door that her quarry was headed toward.

He'd reached the door and pressed against the bar. The door opened, then he realized that there was an unseen barrier which he could not penetrate. Looking around desperately, he wrestled with the idea of taking his victim's life then and there. At that moment, he knew someone was stalking him and he needed every bit of energy he could manage to escape. He'd already spent the last he had to change his appearance to the more youthful aspect.

He tried to press against the barrier but felt a strong reserve of power flowing from the person who'd cast the spell. This showed him who it was that had barred his way.

Following the thread of power back, he spied the woman fighting through the crowd as she tried to reach him. He could see the hatred in her eyes. She was determined and desperate to stop him. It was then he knew he'd seen her before.

Yes, it had been her that ruined his plans. She was becoming a recurring problem. If he managed to get free of her this time he knew he'd need to deal with her. There was no fear in him. He'd done as much before. Every time he tasted the flesh of an adversary he had been fulfilled for many months. There was power in devouring an enemy.

He wondered if she would taste as salty as the last person who'd dared to defy him. Perhaps she was the person he wanted instead. A smile crossed his face, showing his sharp white teeth. He relished the chance to gnaw upon her bones.

Again, he pushed against the barrier she'd erected. This time the feeling of release came as the spell's power had been spent. Rapidly, he exited, dragging his meal along roughly.

The woman followed as they exited through the large glass double door.

The parking garage on the other side of the door stood several stories high. Though well lit, the florescent lights created large pools of dark shadow along the edges of the open space. Each floor contained more than forty cars. Almost every space was taken.

By the time Jamas reached the door, the man and his prey had crossed to an expensive sports car at the far end of the upward sloping ramp.

The man pushed the woman roughly into the passenger seat then began to cross to the driver's side when Jamas caught up to them.

"You can't have her!" she shouted in fluent Japanese. Though she was only a few yards away, the force of her conviction added power to her demand.

"You can't stop me," he replied in English. "She is not yours to protect, witch!" The contempt in his voice was evident.

"I won't let you take her," Jamas interjected. "I will protect her."

"I suspect this is going to get ugly," came the response. "You are half dazed on the dust. Do you really think you have a chance against my power?" he asked.

With that, he stretched forth his hand and pressed his will against that of his adversary.

Jamas said a few words and struck a pose as though she were about to engage in a kung fu fight movie scene. A series of Chinese characters from the sleeve of her right arm disappeared as she finished speaking the words. This engaged her in the battle against the man.

A battle of wills is particularly boring for those that might be viewing the effects. The opponents stand silent and unmoving. It is a staring contest of the mind. Each presses the power of will, its force, against the other. Slowly, meticulously, the being with the stronger will begins to press back against the weaker. If one combatant is a great deal stronger than the other, he or she may force the other to obey their bidding. When equally matched, the results are less spectacular.

This battle was very closely matched. In general, the man had more powerful will, but Jamas had the power of purpose on her side, lending strength. Her conviction of righteousness gave the edge she needed to equal her enemy.

After what seemed like hours but was mere seconds, each knew that a battle of wills would not result in an easy outcome. The man broke it off and took the old route of physical attack.

He closed the gap between the two and leaned into a punch that would have resulted in a contusion of the heart had it connected. Instead, Jamas stepped to the side easily and blocked with her forearm, her hands open and rigid in a knife-like posture. Her legs were wide and her feet perfectly parallel. The angle of her arms was perfectly aligned, fingertips of the left to the elbow of the right.

For less than a heartbeat she froze, waiting for the monster to move. She preferred a defensive posture till she understood his attacking method. The next attack told her all she needed to know.

He spun lightly on his heel and swung a rather unbalanced kick to her midsection.

She slipped back just enough to avoid the clumsy attempt and shifted her arms to the opposite pose. Once the leg swung around, she stepped in behind it and pushed the palm of her left hand into the lower back of the man. The man stumbled backward, off balance.

Jamas followed quickly and slipped a low kick at his now extended leg. Without setting it back down she followed with a kick to his face. Then she leaned into him and drove her right elbow across into his now exposed throat.

He slipped backward in desperation, barely avoiding the attack. As he reached the car, he gripped the door handle and lifted both legs in a rolling motion, flipping back over the car. The effect was to place the car between him and Jamas.

It was obvious now that Jamas was more skilled at hand fighting and this seemed to frighten the man. He looked this way and that seemingly searching for a way to escape. His enhanced physical abilities should have made Jamas an easy target. How could a simple human defeat him?

The answer was simple. Jamas was not a normal human. In fact, she'd studied all her life to fight evil such as this man possessed. He'd called her a witch. Though not technically true, it served as a reminder that she had discipline enough to battle even the likes of him and his fellows.

Fear raged into his eyes as he realized he could not win. Since he'd been changed he had not known fear. His maker had said that darkness was his ally, secrecy his only real weapon. Now both eluded him. He ran.

Jamas was now torn between the need to stop him and the need to help the woman he'd tried to abduct. If the pattern were as she imagined, his evil would already be spreading into her. She decided then to make sure of the safety of the woman before pursuing the man.

She sat in the front seat slumped forward. Jamas checked her pulse and realized that she was still alive but the unsteady and inconsistent beat told her that he'd already begun to infect her.

There are literally dozens of undead creatures in the world. Vampires, ghosts, wraiths, and may more have been created by the forces of evil. Some are tools of the Master, others are simply creatures of evil fighting to survive and feed in a world of the living. There are a few that believe they can regain their humanity by devouring the life force or even the flesh of those that are without corruption. Such is a Wight.

The mentality of the creature is bonded to a recently deceased body. If it feeds on the flesh of the living quickly it can stop the body from rotting away. The legends say that if it consumes enough uncorrupted flesh, the Wight can regain its humanity.

When a person is exposed to the spirit of a Wight, it begins to decay. Slowly the body will die and the person will be faced with the choice: to seek a new body and become a Wight or fade into oblivion. Most good minds realize the truth and chose not to embrace the evil that consumes them. A few chose the chance at life.

The fact that the woman was drunk and unable to form an intelligible thought meant she would probably not understand the choice. She would probably decide to live. Or, really, she would decide not to die. She could then become a terror, feeding on humanity from the shadows.

Jamas had only one spell that might work for this situation. Imprinted on the center seam of her blouse along the line of buttons at the front, was a healing spell. She'd need to adjust it slightly to account for the touch of darkness from the creature.

She would need a little room to perform the required ritual.

Pulling the woman from the car, she placed her in an open area behind it. This was in the line of traffic but it couldn't be helped. There was no other place where she'd have enough room to make the proper mechanics.

In a low stance, she moved. Slowly and precisely, she composed the intentional movements designed to draw out the corrupting influence. The dance of energy seemed almost like the Yang style of Tai Chi. When she lowered into a deep bow stance, her crane's head hand touched just to the left of the heart of the woman. As she rose, a thin line of black and grey smoke rose from the spot and quickly dissipated into nothing.

The woman seemed to breathe easier once the smoke was gone. Color returned to her face and she sighed a soft sigh before pursing her lips and falling into a deep sleep.

The enemy had escaped. Jamas was prepared to wait for him to try again. She knew that he'd move on, though. Now that he was discovered, he'd find a new place to seek his salvation. What the undead do not understand is that nothing can give them back their humanity.

Once tainted, they are forever in the grasp of evil. You can never return from death. The will to live is strong, even in the dead. The need to love, and hope, and touch, is a powerful incentive to do whatever it takes to regain what was lost. The illusion of living is all that is attainable. Part of the natural cycle of life is that we must all die. In death, we consummate our lives. In life, we must accept that death is the last outcome of life.

Jamas realized that she could accept death knowing that, in life, we have done what we could to be the best person we needed to be. What other reason to live than to sacrifice for those we love?

Jamas had let the creature get away. She felt a slight bout of anger over her failure, then realized she'd managed to save the victim. That was something.

For now, she was sure that he'd probably leave Japan for a while. The company's other holdings included offices in London and San Francisco. If she assumed he would try to stay near his financial power base, either could be a possible place to start.

She decided to try California first. It was closer and her brother was studying there. He'd recently asked her if she might find time to help him on a theory he'd been testing, and though he might have already completed his research, she could at least reconnect.

They had been close. Even though they were an ocean apart, their bond was stronger than most siblings. If it turned out to be a waste of time, she could at least enjoy time with Kayle.

# It is Hunger
*Now*

The skull sat in the center of the reading table. Each of the room's occupants stood over it trying to decipher the lines of script patterned into its glossy surface.

A closer examination revealed more than a dozen ancient languages used in unconventional combinations. The gathered team had tried for hours to understand the significance of the talisman. So far none of the theories had proven fruitful.

Nick was joined at the table by Arianna, Conner, Maria, and Lucy. Three of the five were highly educated and seemed to offer the best hope of understanding the skull. Nick and Lucy stood to one side, occasionally offering some input, but generally staying out of the way.

Arianna surmised that there might be another language behind the writing and offered that a phonetics value might be used to develop a natural vocabulary. She'd assigned the phonetics based on the normal linguistic usage for each of the languages present. The Sanskrit and cuneiform were relatively simple, as was the hieratic. For other markings, they'd assumed certain linguistic templates such as first sound for ideograms. This had resulted in an unintelligible bumble of vocalizations that made no sense.

It was Nick who stumbled on the current approach which seemed to be offering better results. Though he was not a trained linguist, he was highly intelligent and the others had come to count on his intuition.

He'd surmised that there was an underlying known language and that the characters where set in a coded way. Some of the oldest codes were simple character replacements. Or one where the characters were jumbled.

The idea that a code might be used with such a diverse array of languages offered the most problematic challenge. How could a person predict what each replacement or order should be?

The answer had to be in the writing on the skull itself. It was Nick that again offered a solution. What if a person deciphered the languages separately? First the hieratic then the Sanskrit, etc. Would the resulting effort translate into some form of intelligible communication?

After several attempts and a few rearrangements based on character order, a picture of the skull was coming into focus.

The plating on the skull was nearly two hundred years old. The polished nickel might have been one of the first objects plated in the early eighteen hundreds. The string of characters that wound around the skull in symmetrical lines were probably carved before the plating process.

Without damaging the skull, it would be difficult to place its origin.

The team had come to learn recently that though many of the languages were thought to be unused for much of history, secret organizations had kept them alive for mystical uses. This made putting a date to the object difficult but not impossible. Now that they had a working translation, it was easier. Certain word usages and the context of the translation showed the skull had been carved about five centuries ago.

The skull was created to relate the story of a man who died and yet still lived by consuming the flesh of the living.

He'd been born on the other end of the world, it said. He had been a man of wealth who travelled from his home to great cities of sixteenth century Europe. He'd visited Paris, Rome, and London. It was on his return journey that he'd stopped in Constantinople.

Taking lodgings with a noble family on the southern shore of the Bosporus, in an old city which was now the Kadikoy district, he spent several weeks exploring the wonders of the ancient city and the surrounding area. He'd travelled along the coast of Asia-Minor before returning suddenly.

An illness had taken him while in Miletus. It was said he'd been attacked by a wild man. Though only slightly injured, his health waned over the next few weeks till he finally succumbed to a sort of cold chill. The sickness didn't seem to be the plague but his death was taken as a bad sign by his Muslim hosts. The body was interred in the catacombs beneath one of the oldest parts of Constantinople.

Though many of the bodies buried here had been dismantled and stacked, his was placed whole in a niche prepared by his host.

Over the next several months, a series of grizzly deaths had occurred near the entrance of the catacomb. After a long witch hunt, it was determined that the night creature was responsible. Though he'd been identified, he had fled before he could be destroyed and had never returned.

A public servant, who had knowledge of the secrets of the gates, created the skull as a warning for generations to follow of the thing the man had become.

A discussion of the nature of the thing began when Arianna and Conner related the translation. What was the nature of such a creature? How would it come into existence? How would it be identified and destroyed?

"It seems to me that it is something like a vampire," Conner said with a slight lisp. "The closest correlation would be something like a Wight. This is an un-living thing that is a cannibal. It consumes living flesh in order to perpetuate its existence."

"It seems a little messy," Maria offered. "I mean, a vampire drinks blood but that could take a relatively short period of time. To consume a whole body could take days or weeks."

"Maybe it's not the actual eating of the flesh, as a whole, that nourishes the creature," Conner replied. "It might be the destruction of life that feeds it. Maybe it's a more metaphysical consuming that occurs. As a Christian consumes the metaphoric body of Christ during the communion, the creature might do something similar. In taking life and consuming flesh it takes empowerment from the transition of life into death."

"The power of transforming life into death might be something akin to opposite particles of matter coming into contact. A sort of antimatter explosion of metaphysical energy?" Arianna offered.

"That is exactly so," Lucy added. "Life is not simply the combination of intellect housed in the brain of a living body. Life is energy that emanates from all things. Though some is contained and separate in the form of individual life, the energy is infinite and omnipresent. People have only just started to touch on the deeper understanding of that energy."

Lucy had a view of the universe that was both deeper and more intrinsic than the others in the room. Not long ago, she had been known as Grieta. She'd been without form. Her mentality had made up a series of gateways between innumerable worlds. She'd given up that form in order to save the universe from a being known as Da Ra Chi Ti. In transitioning to the body of Lucy, she'd opened the way for another to battle the evil one and win. This had resulted in the destruction of the gateways and the connecting rift.

Now she inhabited the body of a woman who'd been near death. The mentality of Lucy had not survived but Grieta managed to save the body and now went by the name of Lucy in honor of the woman whom she could not save. Also, Grieta had access to all the memories of Lucy, which made it somewhat easier for her to assimilate into human life.

She also had memories of ages of observing the working of the universe. She'd become a sort of advisor to the team which now resolved to continue fighting evil in the world.

"The creature is drawing energy from the living at the moment of death. I think it needs a traumatic, gruesome, violent death, to enhance the energy a victim gives. The more powerful the emotion, the greater the nourishment," she added.

"What we are saying is that this thing can extend its 'life' by devouring emotion, not the flesh itself?" Nick asked.

"In a way," Conner interjected. "The thing may not understand the actual mechanic of feeding. Like we normally don't think about how our food is digested. In the case of this thing, it knows a hunger. The hunger is quenched by devouring flesh of a living victim. How that translates into its continued existence is less important than the act of consumption itself."

"It would also explain many of the old legends about vampires and wights. They target the innocent because terror is easier to coax in a young or inexperienced person. The more jaded a person, the less energy they might deliver," Maria added. "I would think that a creature like this would have to be able to generate a lot of radiated fear to enhance the effect. We know that many of the creatures of corruption could do just that."

"I think the correlation is sensible," Lucy added. "It would make sense that living energy is changed by circumstance. Joy, fear, love, hate, all change the experience of life. It would be logical to think that the creature would engender the proper emotional state prior to feeding in order to extract the proper energy."

"I find the discussion a little disturbing," Arianna added. "What you are saying is, there is some logical way a creature whose existence is entirely contradictory to how logic might operate. We've all seen lots of weird things lately but I'm still a little incredulous that there is so simple an explanation for something like this even existing."

"My question is related to her statement," Nick jumped in. "How does something like this thing even come into being in the first place?"

"There are more things in heaven and earth..." Conner smiled. "Who knows?  Maybe the only question we actually have is: how do we destroy it?"

"Thanks for the Shakespeare," Nick smiled back. "Really, that might be the answer to destroying it.  I repeat: how can this thing have come to be?"

Though Nick was a novice in the battle against these otherworldly creatures, he was a quick study.  He'd gone through all the English journals he could over the last few months in an attempt to understand the enemy. He'd also asked Arianna to translate as much as she could about how to battle the creatures they might face.

"Have you read anything about these things?" he asked her.

"Not in anything I've read so far.  I'm not as fast a reader as Chris was.  I'll keep looking but there are still hundreds of books I haven't gone through.  Maria's brother Zach had started a database of the library but it is far from complete. It will take some time, time we may not have."

"So where does that leave us?" Conner jumped in again. "What is the next step?"

"I think I know," Maria interjected. "Jamas was telling us about her trip to Japan right before Father died. I wonder if there is something there that might help."

"Chris was looking through them before he…" Nick trailed off.

"I suppose he could have come across a way to destroy one. If one of these things is still out there then we should probably act," Conner decided.

"That the skull exists in the first place seems to indicate there might be at least one of them out there," Maria added.

"Yes, a cryptic note from one of Conner's friends in England. What was it that she said? An ancient darkness is told in the skull, along with a possible location. It was pretty convenient," Nick offered.

"Well, the first part proved to be true. Maybe we need to get to England and find this friend of yours," Arianna added, nodding to Conner.

"Ok. You trust your friend," Nick nodded to Conner. "I trust my instinct," he said, tapping his chest. "There is something fishy about the whole thing.  It is definitely worth looking into."

Conner's manner had become somewhat aloof since he'd acquired the Keith mentality.  The joining of the two made him a conglomeration of both.  He had memories and attitudes from two lives.  Though he had found it easy to integrate both, his old right hand, Nick, still occasionally found it difficult to relate to the combined personality.  "To England," he finally concurred.

# The Mystic

*3 years ago*

One of the martial arts styles Jamas studied included a philosophy about the useful application of emotion during martial exercises as a method of empowering the artist's actions.

By emoting calm, a person could create a positive defense.  By expressing anger at the right moment, a person could add power to an attack.  By expressing love, a person could endure pain.  Each emotion was useful in a variety of ways.

Jamas had been studying and meditated for more than a year and a half before discovering Oroshi. She decided to returning to California to meet up with Kayle and help him work out a problem he'd uncovered at a bay area university would be a good segue to asking for his help with her won problem.

Kayle parked his older pickup in the arrivals lane.  Jamas stood a few feet back from the curb.  Her dark olive skin and lean frame seemed almost at odds with that of her brother.  She wore the traditional family colors.  At her feet, two small pieces of luggage contained all she needed.  She'd always been a light traveler, and her requirements were minimal.

Kayle jumped out and swung around the truck in easy, rapid motions.  His large muscular frame carried him with a grace that seemed more suited to a dancer than an athlete of his size.

The hug of affection the siblings shared showed a deep connection. As twins, they'd been very close growing up. The few years they'd been separated did in fact make their hearts grow fonder.

Since finishing college, Jamas had been on a personal journey, travelling the orient and studying a variety of martial arts styles. She'd also visited several families involved in the battle against corruption and learned many of their beliefs and techniques. She'd only returned to aid Kayle in his own investigations.

Kayle was working on his masters in evolutionary biology. Though he had a full athletic scholarship, in three years he'd finished his undergrad work. With another year of eligibility, he pursued the next level of his education.

During his research, he'd discovered that humanity had evolved from several lines of prehuman descendants. Though many had been identified, species such as Homo Erectus and Denisovan, there were at least three that had, as yet, not been identified.

Kayle had been working on the theory that life evolves in similar ways in similar conditions. This was an extension of the parallel evolution ideas that had been presented in the early days of the science. His work broadened those ideas to include not only simply similar environments, but also identical worlds. These theories would never be published for the outside world but they could enhance the family understanding of the rift and its purpose.

Jamas tossed her bags in the bed of the truck and climbed in. Kayle pulled away and started down the ramp that would lead to the highway and back toward the city. The distant light glittered brightly in the early morning darkness.

"Thanks for coming," Kayle said with a smile. "I thought this was more up your alley than mine."

"You have a mystery that you can't solve and decided I was a better candidate as chief investigator?" Jamas asked.

"Well, in the interest of fair competition, I felt I should bring you in on it," Kayle responded. "You would have hated to be left out of this one."

"Good. I have a mystery I'd like to talk to you about as well. First yours then mine," she insisted.

"We are on our way to my mystery. We could discuss yours on the way," Kayle was always the gentleman.

The two had similar competitive spirits. Throughout their childhood, they competed in pretty much every athletic endeavor. Often that spilled over into the academic. By bringing Jamas in on his own investigation, Kayle was reinstituting the sibling rivalry.

At some point a series of rules would be set down so that each would be on equal footing. Competition needed organization. Rules ensured that each participant was evaluated in a fair and unbiased way. Rules for action and a clear set of goals were required in order to frame the activity in a way that could engage each competitor.

Since Kayle had called her, he would create the framework of the competition. Normally it would give him the advantage. Kayle was the ultimate sportsman, though. He would ensure that Jamas had an equal chance in the investigation that was coming.

She felt it important that he set the rules as her quest was of an entirely different nature to her own. First though, she needed to frame her part of the competition in a way that would allow him to generate reasonable, balanced, and fair conditions for whatever challenge was agreed upon.

"Well, my problem is a little weird but pretty cool. There is an undead monster hunting people for food. I think I know the generalities and have several methods of fighting it but, I feel like I missed my first chance at stopping it and thought we could tackle it together," she offered in an unembarrassed tone. Working together on a real challenge always invigorated both of them.

"Ok," he replied.  Look, maybe yours is more important but mine can be done quickly.  Let's tackle mine first and then go after whatever you are tracking."

"Fine.  After your thing I want to check in with some friends.  I'm hoping they can tell me more about what we are after." Jamas was feeling better about her chances now that Kayle was going to help.

Kayle had an apartment near campus.  The one bedroom edifice was expensive but he enjoyed his privacy and, as a graduate student athlete, he was allowed the indulgence.

Jamas was set up on the couch.  After her shower, they talked for a while to catch up.  By 3:00 AM they retired.

In the morning, the two spoke over breakfast.  Kayle laid out his plan.  Then he set the rules.

"You are firstly a martial artist but your degree is in oriental studies," he began.  "I've come across several things which seem to support my theories.  There are, however, quite a few inconsistencies in practical application.  For instance, I've identified several specific genetic markers whose origin I cannot discover.  These have been introduced maybe a half dozen times in unrelated or isolated parts of the world.  The most recent seems to have been around fifteen hundred years ago in the southwest.  The earliest might be fifty-five thousand years ago in Australia."

"I'm not a biologist," Jamas responded. "How can I possibly help with your study?"

"First, this isn't a biology study. I'll explain in a minute. Second, you are uniquely qualified to help. Of all the family, you are the only one that genetically expressed our Native American heritage in a significant way. Those markers are in all of the family but did not express except in you. That is, of course, part of the nature of genetics."

"Each of us in the family has unique talents and skills. These are perfected by practice but ingrained in our basic makeup. Certainly, nurture and nature both play a part. The basic postulation is, how do people who are genetically so very similar and live in essentially the same state of nurture, end up being so unique? Is there some depth of the basic human genome that might be responsible for the individual diversity? Is it simply that some small percentage of genetic divergence means so much in terms of the final disposition of the individual?"

"Still not following," Jamas interrupted. "What are you getting at?"

"In a minute," Kayle replied. "Here is the thing. You and I are twins. We have as much in common as any of those in the family and yet we still are very divergent in so many ways. Those three things: genetics, nurture, and our individual experience makes us who we are."

"What if there is another element to that?" he asked. "What if destiny or fate also paves the way for our potentials to be realized?  What if, as so many theologians insist, there is a predetermined, non-genetic mechanism involved?"

"How could you possibly test for that?" Jamas asked. "What metric could you use to even qualify a person's predetermination for a personality type?"

"That is the question," he said in an excited tone.  The smile told Jamas he was about to get to the point.

"I met someone," Kayle began.

"You think it's destiny to fall for that person?" Jamas smiled.

"No.  Not that," he continued.  "This woman came in for one of the genetic studies.  I took the sample and was about to usher her out when she said something that gave me a start.  She told me that I should get my twin and come to see her.  She gave me her address and insisted that she could shed some light on our family business."

"At first I was taken back.  Then she told me that it would be our fate to die soon.  She said she could see that much.  Perhaps together we might be able to avoid the death that was coming," his smile widened.

"Of course, I thought she was pulling my leg. The more I thought about it, the more I felt that if it were even slightly possible that she might be right, I wanted to take the precaution. If I could prevent your death, then I should. But more than that, I began to think in terms of fate. I'm sure that Zach would have come up with some really pretty way of metaphorizing the idea. For me, I felt that this might provide an opportunity to study why someone believes in predetermination."

"Not strictly speaking my field. Really more Zach's. At any rate, I began to put my theory to the problem. Genetic propensity, nurture, experience, or fate might be a determinant in our deaths that could be predicted by a person that neither you nor I'd ever met."

"Ok. You framed the problem. How do we prove any of what you said? I mean, are we trying to give some kind of percentage of each to categorize the potential influence it might have or simply trying to prove that fate is a real thing?" she asked.

"In our family business, we sort of assume fate as a given. But, is what this person says real? That we will die soon is such an ominous thing to have hanging. It brings out the other side of the question which is maybe more pertinent. Having been warned of our fate, can we change it?" Kayle asked.

"Too many questions for a single study I think," Jamas responded. "Our real goal is simply: does this person believe in fate and how do they get their information?"

"We could start by simply listening. After that we can decide if it is worth pursuing," Kayle continued.

"If it were anyone else I would have been angry for bringing me all this way. As it is, I felt the need to go home. After we are done here, that's what I intend to do. You always do bring me the best questions Kayle."

They arranged to meet the seer later that evening in her own home. She lived on a steep street in the heart of the city. The house was a tall but narrow three story affair. Its clapboard siding was white but the accent elements were of a dark brown. A large single round window centered the upmost floor. The small front yard was covered in what looked like AstroTurf. The California drought had taken its toll on landscaping in recent years.

Jamas paid the cab and followed her brother to the tall six panel door. The upper four panels contained frosted glass while the larger lower two panels were dark mahogany stained wood. The framing of the door was of a slightly lighter wood. Kayle used the knocker centered in the cross of the upper four panels.

The sound of footsteps indicated that the home was largely uncarpeted. The sound of heels on the hardwood floors rapped out a staccato that slowly increased till the door swung open.

A thin woman in her early fifties smiled at the siblings. Without a word, she motioned them into her home. Her footsteps were now joined by the softer clap made from the soft athletic shoes of the pair.

Jamas inspected the woman. She was medium height and slightly built. She wore a somewhat modern sundress but it was obviously not ironed. The wrinkles also indicated she probably didn't hang the dress but had tossed it haphazardly into a drawer. Her shoes were simple black heals. Though they added an inch of height, she was still not imposing. Her light brown frizzled hair had begun to grey.

As they entered the parlor at the back of the house, the woman asked them to sit. Several antique chairs and a sofa stood in careful disarray. Two cats curled against each other in a pet bed near a fireplace that had been converted to gas. Additional heat radiated through the windows at the back which faced the setting sun. This made the house quite warm. The siblings both felt comfortable and welcome.

"I was hoping you could make it here. It's not long coming. And when I met you at that science thing I knew it was you who I'd seen." She seemed eager to get the conversation rolling.

**Sell your books at World of Books!**
Go to sell.worldofbooks.com and get an instant price quote. We even pay the shipping - see what your old books are worth today!

Inspected By: eliazar_cucul

00082184866

"This is your sister, then." A statement, not a question. "She is just like I imagined from my vision."

"Vision?" Kayle asked.

"Dream really," she informed him. "But when they are vision dreams, that's what I call them, they always seem deeper, more deliberate. At any rate, I write those ones down. Or at least as much as I can remember. They fade quickly. Like all dreams, I guess."

"What can you tell us about the vision?" Jamas was always eager to get to the point.

"Simply that someone who was loved more than anything will kill you. And someone you never met will free you."

"That's it?" Jamas was not impressed.

"No, that's not it," the woman smiled. "I wrote it down. It's my scratching so you probably can't read it. I'll tell you what it says."

"The dream took me to a house covered in words from the past. Words that could not be translated. Words that had power beyond imagining. Inside the house, the brothers and sisters began to die after the stranger came. They were killed not by him but by someone who was the ghost of the past, a dead reminder that anything can be corrupted. The stranger fought the monster and won. But only one other survived. She who is with child will prepare the way to the future. Your sister I think. She lives in sadness. She who has lost all will regain all. There is a cycle of things. Karma if you will. That which is given will be returned. That which is taken will be reborn." She stopped and fell silent.

After a moment Kayle asked "What can we do to prevent this from happening?"

"Knowing the possibilities can offer you many alternatives. The only way I can see making things different is to act before it happens. Perhaps if you find the stranger before things unfold. The stranger is the key. But be warned, he is without connection. He cannot understand what you ask. Like the card of the tarot, he is the fool."

"What does this stranger look like? Who is he?" Jamas asked.

"I don't remember. I only know he was shrouded in a soft sparkle of blue and silver. He may come as a seeker of thing hidden. He may come without knowing his destiny. The feeling I got was one of sadness and pain. Recent loss. Life spent without purpose. There is a rain which comes with him. A rain which will cleanse. He is coming alone for he will always be alone. And because of his aiding you, he will also die. He will wither and fade then die by his own choice. Not right away. It will be a lingering death. The death of the stranger will mean the end of the long struggle. It will be the beginning of a new battle, though.  There is never an empty space that is not filled.  There must always be balance."

*Figure 2 Nordhamshin Estate*

# Across Atlantic

*Now*

The marshes of the lowlands in England are usually cold and dreary during winter. This winter had been no different. A fog had crept across the long valley and only a small swatch of trees stood tall enough to break the grey cotton like layer which seemed to billow with each small wind like the breathing of a gigantic dragon. The forecast indicated a storm was on the way and though the landscape seemed bleak, it would undoubtedly be worse soon.

Nick looked out across the landscape and wondered. Things seem to have gotten off to a good start here but there was a level of discomfort as the team had found itself staying at the Nordhamshin estate.

Keith Nordhamshin was one half of the person now known to the public as Conner Duran. They'd decided to keep the family from knowing the truth behind Keith/Conner.

The estate was large. In the old days, it might have been staffed by dozens of the servant class. Modern times and sensibilities had reduced the number to only five.

Nick's room had two windows. One facing east over the moor and one south looking down on the large garden which made the front of the estate. The room also featured a large four poster bed which was too soft for

Nick.  Along one wall stood a thin side table with a basin and pitcher.  Above that a round mirror offered a reflection.  The other wall was interrupted only by the door which led to the long hallway which made the main feature of this wing of the home.  Traditional wood and wallpaper finishes completed the anachronism which was better placed at least a hundred years in the past.

He stood at one window enjoying a quintessential English morning.  Somehow it was not depressing him in any way.  He almost felt like he could hear the hound calling its baleful cry of fate.

A knock at the door brought him back from his Baskerville fantasy.  He crossed the room quickly but quietly and opened the door to find Conner and Maria.  He stepped aside to give them room to enter.  Conner shook his head and said in a low tone.  "Actually, I thought we should discuss the next step over breakfast," he smiled and waved his hand in an inviting gratuity.

"Sure.  I'll be down in a minute," Nick responded.

"The main dining room.  We'll all be waiting," Conner offered.

Once alone, Nick quickly brushed his teeth using the basin and water to rinse.  Then he adjusted his belt line and ran his hand down his shirt and checked himself in the mirror to ensure that he was free of wrinkles and loose threads.  He tapped each toe to the floor to knock off the loose dust which could not have settled in the time since he put on the oxfords.

Nick was not a superstitious person.  He was, however, very meticulous in his habits.  Honed by several years in the Army he continued to repeat this ritual even though he knew no one would inspect the results.  Only after he completed the required adjustments would he head down to meet the others.

Maria, Conner, Lucy, and Arianna had already begun breakfast.  Though the long table had been set up for several guests, only the three were present when Nick entered the room.

He crossed to the sideboard and assembled a plate of eggs and sausage.  A decanter held orange juice which he poured into a waiting glass.  He finished his placement by requisitioning coffee from a large stainless electric percolator which decanted from a spout at the bottom.

Though the rest of the team had been talking while he built his meal, they reserved the topic of the trip till he sat and began to eat.

"We have the translation.  We have the skull.  My friend will be here later today to enlighten us about the meaning of both," Conner said in a dry tone.

Nick had still not gotten used to the weird accent which combined Texas with British in a way that almost made him sound Australian. It was the odd lisp he still carried that disrupted what might have been a clear impression of the man he hoped was still in there somewhere.

It seemed odd that he would feel such disconnection for Conner. For several years, they'd been the closest of friends and had faced danger a dozen times together. The man he'd become was different and at the same time just as he thought he should be. Conner was a smart pass, not an academic. Now though, he was both.

Still, Conner paid him. He was, if nothing else, a damn good employee. There were still many things he enjoyed about the job. Some people might have thought Nick to be a danger junkie. That wasn't true at all. He did enjoy doing a good job though. It simply turned out that he was very good at the job he was doing. Danger was just a large part of that job.

"What we have learned so far is that the skull seems to have been created as a warning against some ancient evil creature. As we all know, the loss of the gates has cut off evil from other worlds but not stopped evil that was already in our world. I believe we are facing something that has been here for some time. Perhaps one of the archetypical evils which have always been part of human culture," Maria continued.

"We have decided it is something akin to a Wight. A thing that feeds on the living to keep the appearance of life. The question we are asking is, is this thing real? More important than that, is it still a threat?"

"I did some work on Jamas' journal. I was aware that Chris had been reading these when he disappeared. Though a few are missing, the ones I was able to read through show that she and Kayle had faced off against something very much like this only a couple of years ago. What happened is not recorded. Maybe it was in the journals that are missing? At any rate, there seems to be a correlation,"

At this point, Conner took up the story.

"If my friend was attempting to tell us that the thing is real and a threat we should find out soon and be able to take action. It is my belief that a creature such as this would want to remain in the shadows. Its best defense is to remain unknown and undiscovered. According to tradition, there are several weapons against such a thing as this. But to be clear, the word itself is really a derivation of the old English Wiht. I decided to use it in an unconscious nod to literary references that describe an undead creature that devours the life force by consuming the flesh of the living."

"By way of destruction, we can use fire for certain. Our recent endeavors show we should be able to dismember it and therefore render it powerless. Since it is a dead creature, it will probably rot away if it cannot feed. I would also assume that destruction of any vital organ will render it dead just as doing so will cause a living person to die.  One challenge might be that minor injuries may have little or no effect.  Another question has come up.  If it can regenerate its body by using the life force of its prey, then it might be able to repair damage from any number and type of wounds using the same power," Conner cocked his head in a thoughtful way.  "It might be damned difficult to deal with."

"So, we have just as little real information about this than we have had about everything else we have faced so far?" Nick asked.

"Just so," Conner agreed.

"When is your friend expected to arrive?" Lucy asked.

"She should be here around noon.  She called just before she left Oxford.  She was afraid she might not beat the storm on her way up," Conner confirmed.  "She is also an academic.  Her field is history and cultures.  Though she holds a professorship at the women's college, her real passion lies in the library.  She is one of the eminent researchers at Oxford," Conner smiled in pride at the thought of his friend.  "She is also my niece.  I have taken to referring to her as my friend because of my current identity issue."

"How did she know you were still alive?" Arianna asked.

"The oddness of circumstance actually. She was a friend of Doris, Maria's aunt. It was through her that Doris and Maria came to the excavation in Asia. After that trouble and my subsequent reintegration into my current life, Doris had unwittingly informed her I still lived. She investigated and we have since become pen pals of a sort," Conner smiled.

"She can be trusted then?" Nick asked.

"I think that goes without saying," Conner nodded.

The rest of the morning was spent discussing recent discoveries. Though no new information had been forthcoming, the team seemed to use the time to continue to bond. Since the death of Chris Jensen, they'd been somewhat listless and without direction. Having a solid goal seemed to be refreshing to each. The goal unified them in their mission.

It was nearly one thirty before Conner's niece arrived. Traffic from the city had been heavier than usual. The group again commandeered the large dining room for a meeting.

Conner introduced his friend to the group. "This is Jenny. Jenny this is Nick, Lucy, and Arianna. You remember Maria of course."

"So good to meet all of you," Jenny replied, taking each hand in turn and offering vigorous affection through the greeting.

They each took a seat at the table. The team used only one end of the dozen foot long dark walnut antique. The skull stood silent testament to the gathering of minds.

"I had read," Jenny began, "about the skull while studying strange incidents in Asia Minor. After learning of Keith and the nature of his...rescue...I felt I could turn my powers of research to good use. There are literally thousands of volumes related to the occult and supernatural at Oxford. I thought perhaps I could learn more about what Keith was facing."

"When I discovered he was alive I sought him out. Doris was very honest about the Drakson family and its business. Turns out that it took very little time to find many references to ancient evil in the world," she continued.

"The reason the skull seemed important was that it was the first one where there was a recent modern mention. About ten years ago, it had been stolen from the vaults of a museum in Venice. The events surrounding the theft caused me to send my somewhat cryptic note."

"Several desiccated bodies had been discovered the night the skull disappeared. These were later identified as the night guards at the museum. Though each appeared to have been mummified for centuries, the men had been alive only a few hours before discovery. This and the fact that large sections of their flesh had been torn off by what the coroner described as animal teeth."

"After more research, I discovered a similar item had been shipped to Africa by a noted collector of occult objects. It happens out to have been the same skull you have here. I was able to identify it by checking insurance manifests for the shipping company. The collector avoided discovery by shipping it from France and listing it as a book end. There had been a photo taken, however, and that was how I knew it to be the same."

"I looked into the collector. He turned out to be something of a mystery. Until a few years ago, he was a real nobody. He is a Belgian by birth. He'd been a laborer at a computer factory in Asia for some years. In only a short time he came into millions of pounds, retired, and purchased the estate in Africa. The local government seemed to be protecting him from some international inquiry which seems to have been dogging him. He'd chosen the country because of its distrust of international interference. A sort of diplomatic shield."

"Just last week, his body was discovered. He seems to have been killed by lions and partially devoured. This would have been some few days after you came into possession of the skull," she finished.

# San Francisco

*3 years ago*

The early morning fog clung lazily to the hills which climbed upward from the bay. Tall homes stood side by side like steps in a giant staircase leading steeply upward. Some white or pale blue, others in darker colors representing the personal tastes of the owners. Although the street was steep, cars lined both sides of the residential street. Tires turned to the curb to keep them from rolling down should the brakes fail.

Jamas was dressed in a tight fitting running outfit. The late winter chill necessitated the use of gloves and a cap to help keep in what body heat she could. The black spandex was interrupted by pink stripes on the outer thigh and shoulders. She ran rapidly up the hill puffing deeply to fill her lungs for the climb.

At each corner, she stopped and dropped to a pushup position to do fifty before continuing upward at a fast sprint. Another two miles and she would return to the hotel and run through her martial arts forms. Her mind was on her plans for later. She wanted to spend time in the Asian district. Chinatown.

She'd developed many connections in the area over the last few years. One family had been dispossessed of the need to watch over a gate in their homeland by a dam whose foundations and flood now blocked the entrance of a gateway. These friends were well respected in the area and knew much of ancient lore pertaining to her vocation. They might have information she could use in her continued search for the fiend that had recently escaped her.

Jamas was also planning on spending time with her brother Kayle who was attending university in the bay area. He'd completed his initial grad level work and had been involving himself in several studies into paranormal and supernatural abilities. His athletics would keep him from joining her for a few days while the wrestling team was at a tournament.

She knew he'd be back by the end of the weekend and wanted to have the business part of her trip out of the way before then so she could enjoy being with her twin.

Jamas was the first of the twins to come into the world. She and Kayle, born only moments apart, had been inseparable for most of their childhood. She had a darker toned skin all her life. The genetics from her native American heritage also expressed themselves in a strong willed independent youth.

She never crossed the line when it came to discipline. Her nature was strict self-focus and awareness. Her desire to be good at everything she did was a powerful and unforgiving compulsion.

From the time she could walk, she was running and practicing athletic skills. Her agility, strength, endurance, eye hand coordination, and technical skill continued to keep everyone one else one step behind, except Kayle.

There are those twins who for whatever reason become polar opposites. There are those that have a great deal of similarity. In the case of Jamas and Kayla, they had the same drive and focus and athletic ability. They drove each other to the brink, and reveled in each other's accomplishments. Jamas would place first at a track meet, and Kayle would win a golden gloves tournament. She would earn her black belt, he would lead his team to a championship. They were always in competition, and at the same time completely enjoying each other's success.

Their personalities meshed well and even though brother and sister, they shared their lives without regard for the difference in sex. Each trusted the other implicitly. Whatever secrets one had, the other knew. When Jamas had a crush on someone, Kayle would be told and asked for advice. When Kayle felt self-conscious about his looks, Jamas would provide comfort. So much of their lives were intertwined and yet at the same time they had different ways of dealing with things.

Kayle was even tempered and quiet. He kept his opinions to himself unless he felt strongly. His focus and intensity for athletic competition was the only place he externally showed emotion. From calm to aggressive in a moment, then back as soon as the action was over.

Even during the most hotly contested competition he could be calm between storms.

Jamas was more outspoken and even somewhat hotheaded. She could steam up into a rage quickly and for the duration of any competitive event, be energized. Between matches at the martial arts competitions she would pace and fritter. She couldn't wait to get into the fray. That is not to say she was out of control. She used emotion to provide energy for her activities. She could stir it up and channel it into her competitive need. It would always take her time to wind down though.

When competing against each other, they would be nearly unstoppable. Sometimes hours and hours of physical competition would ensue over a simple claim that one of them was better at a certain style of fencing.

They played by the rules in every competitive endeavor. They would be absolutely intent on making sure that they knew, understood, and followed them to the tee. Rules are not made to be broken. It is how they know that whatever playing field, or mat, or court, they were on, they would be judging each other, or their competition, based on real strengths and weaknesses. Although they didn't win every time they competed, they always followed the rules. They nearly always won.

It was after high school that they finally went out on their own. Kayle when to a university in the west and Jamas went on to study in Asia.

Jamas spent 3 years in Japan and another 4 years in China studying martial arts and culture under a variety of masters. She became a qualified instructor in 6 different martial arts styles during her stay in the east. She also competed regularly as a way of testing her skills against the best martial artists the world had to offer.

Her focus on study was less about martial arts and more about the history and tradition of each style. Most of the older traditional styles were steeped in mystery and spiritual awareness. The combination of the physical and the mystical excited her.

As she got older, she realized there was very little in the realm of the physical she couldn't accomplish. She became naturally attracted to the spirituality related to physical activities. Her study of traditional martial arts was particularly exciting because of the combination of mystical and physical. This became especially evident when she began studying the internal styles such as Tai Chi, Paqua, and Hsing-I.

During her studies, she found a teacher of an old family style that combined many of the internal styles with a form of alchemical mysticism. The practitioners were also the family that guarded the now buried gate in China. There she learned new spells and forms that helped her to a new and exciting level of understanding her own family heritage.

When she returned home, she put her new knowledge to use right away, testing the useful nature of each thing she had discovered. In a short while she had added two volumes to the library on alternate methods of interpreting the nature of the corruption.

The current question was about the nature of evil her new adversary seemed steeped in. Her brother had inferred that evil took many forms and that corruption might not be the only expression of evil in our world. She began to wonder how the master created and utilized his brand of corruption. Perhaps this new enemy had no connection to either the gates or the master.

There are old legends that indicate evil might be from a single source. Some believe that the devil is the only generator of evil intent and that, even though people can be swept up in it, it is not inherent in the human condition. There are other theologies which teach that evil is part of the natural course of things. In this ideology, a person should seek balance so that both the good and the evil are bound to the other.

Throughout history there had always been an understanding of the war between these polar natures. Jamas didn't care how a philosopher might define either. Her only concern was the task. Her job. To defend our world from unnatural forces. In her mind, evil was to be battled and that was that.

Her current quarry was evil. She had no doubts. He was therefore a target for her attention.

Her morning martial practice was uninterrupted. Once the bed was moved to the end of the large suite, she began. She'd stayed in a calm, focused, mental state while she ran through all the motions she could, given the area of the room. Once completed, she meditated for an hour before showering.

Kayle picked her up in his beat up pickup. They chatted about family and recent events as he drove toward the downtown area of San Francisco.

Their next stop was a restaurant near the center of Chinatown just off Kearny street. The Rainbow Dragon had been purchased only fifteen years ago by the current owners. Though the family had only been in the bay area for less than twenty years, they were well respected ambassadors of traditional Asian culture.

The grandfather in the family had started a martial arts school a few blocks north. It was there that Jamas had studied the ancient arts of the Wu Xian Kwan. The five elements style was as mystical as it was effective. Practitioners studied the traditions of five animal Kung Fu. They were also indoctrinated in the five elements and how each could be manipulated.

Jamas sought out Chun who ran the school. He had a great deal of experience and knowledge regarding corruption and how to fight it.

He was a short but sturdy man in his later sixties. The Xuéxiào school where she'd learned from Chun was rather traditional in its style. A square of structure enclosed the open central training area. To the rear was the private teaching area which held a variety of weapons and wall hangings dedicated to the style.

On one wall was a scroll which presented the lineage of the style. Nineteen generations of masters had presided over the tradition. The final student had been Min. She'd been married to a westerner only a year before. Her school was in Albuquerque.

Jamas had studied here for nearly seven months before being sent on to China for further instruction. Though she could have remained here and learned more from Chun, he felt her aptitude might be in another style.

Chun and Jamas had maintained a very fond friendship, though. Chun had thought of her as his own family. Jamas respected Chun as she did her own father.

Jamas sat cross-legged. Her hands rested respectfully on her knees. She waited quietly till Chun entered the room from the opposite side. She introduced her brother but remained seated. Chun nodded then moved over to a dark lacquered sideboard where a silver platter waited with a service of herbal tea.

Kayle remained silent, sitting in a similar position to Jamas' left. Though he would listen to the entire conversation, he knew that this was something she had started. For that reason alone, she should take the lead. There was never any feeling of jealousy between the two. Each implicitly trusted and respected the other.

They waited as Chun poured tea for each in turn. Then Chun sat directly across from Jamas in the position of honor. It was not meant as a display of dominance. It was meant as a respect for the traditions of the style.

Once Chun was seated, both waited till asked about their health. He also specifically wanted to know what Jamas had been up to. Instead of getting to the point of her visit, she asked after Chun and his family. Finally assured that the formal requirements had been met, she asked him about the Wight.

"I met a man," she said. "He was not a living man. He fed on the flesh of the living to keep the appearance of living. I used a spell that my brother created to see into his corruption. The result was confusing. My brother thinks that he is not a servant of the Master. I think he might be a sort of free agent. I do believe him to be evil, though. I was hoping you could shed some light on what I'm facing."

"Goeng-si. These are the unburied. There are many stories of them. What is it that I can tell you?" Chun asked.

"How to fight them for one," Jamas quickly responded. "But, how do I find them? What are the signs? Can you tell me how to track it down and destroy it?"

"Yes. There are many stories of these things. They feed on the chi of the living. At the very moment of death, fear and terror enhance the flesh with energy. It is this that they feed on. This keeps them young and supple. If they cannot feed, they become stiff and like a corpse, they cannot bend their limbs. Once engorged on the chi they need, they can become young and beautiful. It is an abomination to suffer the living so the dead can walk the world," Chun explained.

"Many stories are told of how they come to be. A person might not have had a proper burial. Maybe it is because they are effected by another Goeng-si. One thing that is always true: there is a choice. Once a person knows that they might become a creature of darkness, they must choose to fight for darkness or for light. If for light they move on to the next life. If they chose for darkness, then they must feed on the living energy of people to survive."

"There are many things that can deal destruction to one of their kind. Fire, for it consumes the flesh. Time, without feeding the body will eventually rot away.

Jujube is an effective deterrent. Since they are less powerful during the daylight hours, the call of a rooster is said to send them scurrying for shelter. They shy away from the sign of the Ba Gua and from the sound of a hand bell."

"It is said that a person who is attacked by one of these creatures may be able hold their breath so that the creature cannot draw from them the essence which is their chi energy. Chi is breathed in and out from the center like a mighty powerful wind. By holding your breath, it is said, that you will hold back the chi by stopping the movement of it within your body. I am not sure that will work though."

"These are only stories. I have never come across one of them. I wonder, is this creature an Asian man?"

"Yes, Japanese I think," Jamas wondered at the question. "Why?"

"Every culture has their own demons. What you think he is from a western point of view may not be right. And though Japanese and Chinese culture has a similar foundation, it is not the same. You should confer with the Togogura family. They would be able to offer a more accurate version of what this thing is that you are hunting," Chun replied.

"I am proud of you my student," he changed the subject. "You have surpassed my expectations and I am honored to have been able to know you." He smiled.

"Thank you," Jamas replied. "How do I find the Togogura clan?"

"The Togogura family is an old family that now has descendants in the area. I will arrange a meeting for you. Be careful, they know of the battle between the opposing furies of light and darkness but they do not take sides. Though they have great knowledge of things related to our work, they can work against the light sometimes."

"We will have to convince them to help us," Jamas said in a sure and confident tone.

"That might not be easy. The only thing they respect more than tradition, is strength," Chun replied.

Jamas smiled "I'm strong."

Chun smiled in return.

*Figure 3 The Chapel*

# Deciphering Death
*Now*

Nick did not believe in chance. He'd spent most of his career planning and observing and understanding the situation and responding accordingly. Only lately had his faith in the power of a good plan been challenged. Several of his most detailed plans had been derailed by circumstances he'd failed to account for adequately.

Recently he'd come to believe he must rely on judgement and experience to get him through the worst failures he had ever been part of.

He felt the mission to Asia had been a failure even though the team was successful in securing the now useless gateway between worlds. There had been many deaths which he felt personally responsible for and he carried the weight of them with him still.

The loss of the group's leader also weighed heavily on him. It was Chris's choice, of course, but Nick thought himself responsible for protecting every team member. He was also aware that Chris was capable of taking care of himself. The worst part was the feeling he was inadequate or incapable of doing what was required of him.

Nick's skillset was growing, though. He had no real skill at spell making. He tried a little and found he didn't have the proper mindset. He was still a very capable soldier.

Over the last few months, he had expanded his knowledge of creatures he had no idea existed until recently. Finding mundane ways of dealing with them had become something of a crusade. He'd spent hours and hours in the library reading every book he could without translation. Though he was studying many of the older languages and had made good progress, he asked Arianna to translate sections that seemed important.

He felt he was finally starting to fit into the team. The others were all academics and geniuses. Though Nick was highly intelligent, he would never be at home in many of the discussions they engaged in.

Finding that Conner was now among them caused further angst. Not long ago Conner and Nick had been intellectual equals. With the combined memories of Keith and Conner, he could not keep up.

Still, Nick was competent at his job. His ability as a man of action in a team composed mostly of intellectuals made him all the more important. Once in a while he might need reinforcements. He could call on other friends if needed.

The security company that he and Conner started was running itself. Though small, the dozen employees were all well versed in the problems of the group. Each was a skilled veteran of military or police groups from around the world. Lately there had been little need of them.

The group had been interred at the Nordhamshin estate for several days. Poor weather and the renewed connection to Conner/Keith's niece had given the group a chance to relax some. Both to wait for the now heavily snowed roads to be cleared and to further discuss the mystery of the metal skull.

Many of the conversations had bordered on the bizarre and though Nick had become good at hiding it, he'd been as often confused as not. Again, it didn't sit well with him. Both the inaction and the constant discussion seemed to be grating on his nerves. He continued to tell himself to be patient. Sooner or later action would be the order and he would be ready.

The night was somewhat bright as the light from a nearly full moon diffused through the clouds and reflected upon the snow-covered ground. As he looked out the frosted window of his bedroom, Nick saw a pale glow that seemed to come from an area some mile and a half from the house. This would have been just at the edge of the moor which surrounded the higher ground upon which both roads and homes stood.

At first he thought it must be an illusion brought on by the strange shadows and the weird atmosphere. Then it moved. It seemed to glide along the edge of the grasses which thrust up through the snow. A sparkling of light played along the pale white glow as it left what appeared to be foot prints in the now disturbed winter blanket.

Nick turned and ran downstairs carefully. At the bottom of the stairs he turned to the right and entered the large drawing room where the academic contingent of the group continued to explore possible meanings in the skull.

"There is a light outside," Nick expulsed. "It's darn cold out there. The wind is up. If someone is stuck out in that they could easily be in trouble."

Conner stood and frowned. Nick wouldn't make a joke of danger. "What did you see?" he asked.

"There seemed to be a light, or a glow. At first I thought it might be just some strange play of light on the snow but then I saw it move. There were definitely tracks in the snow," Nick replied as he pulled on the heavy coat he'd hung on a rack near the french door which led to a patio behind the house.

Without waiting for anyone to comment he opened the door and stepped out. As he pulled the door closed, Conner caught up and tore his own coat from the rack.

Conner called to the others as he followed. "Stay here. Nick and I will check it out."

They crossed to a set of stairs which lead to a garden area behind the large home. From there they followed a gravel pathway which ran around to both sides. Nick led them to the left. Once off the path, they found the going somewhat slowed by the calf high snow drift which had set in the day before.

"About a mile out!" Nick yelled. "This way." He used his hand to point in the direction of travel. Conner followed about two meters behind. Both men were somewhat slouched as they pushed through the resistant ground cover.

The wind had begun to howl in earnest as they got closer to the edge of the moor. On occasions when they felt inclined to converse they were required to yell at the top of their lungs. After an eternity of trudging one foot after the other, Nick stopped and lifted a fist.

Conner stopped instantly.

Ahead of them Nick saw a trail of snow pushed wide. The person that had made the trail must have been very large. From his previous vantage, it seemed whoever it had been had been moving to the right of where Nick and Conner now stood.

Nick turned into the trail knowing that it would be easier to follow in the path already made. Conner stepped in behind him and, though they moved quicker, they were both still very cautious. Every now and then the clear sign of a pair of human looking shoeprints were evident at the bottom of the track.

After several hundred yards, they came to a stop. The trail in the snow had ended without any sign of the person who made it.

Nick turned back to Conner and informed him of the situation in a series of yells. "THE TRAIL ENDS... HERE... MAYBE I WENT THE... WRONG WAY..."

"LET'S TRY BACK THE WAY WE CAME," Conner replied.

Conner took the lead as they retraced their steps. The cold seemed to be getting colder and though it was no longer snowing, the sides of the trail had begun to fall into the trench making it less easy to traverse. As they crossed the intersection where they had entered the path, they both began to feel wary.

After another fifty yards Conner stopped and turned to indicate they'd reached the end.

"NOTHING HERE... WHAT COULD HAVE HAPPENED TO THE PERSON THAT MADE THIS TRACK?"

Nick shook his head. "THERE'S NOTHING WE CAN DO. BEST TO GET BACK AND TRY A SEARCH IN THE MORNING."

Once inside they stripped off their coats and stood near the fire rubbing their hands to spread the warmth as quickly as they could. It was Conner that informed the others about the aborted search.

"We did find a track of someone that seemed to parallel the moor. After a quick search, we could find no one. No sign of the person other than the track itself. There was no way a person could have left that, and not any other indication of where they had gone. Both ends of the trench stopped dead without any other sign."

"It's been going on an hour now that Nick said he saw someone. Could anyone survive that long in the cold out there?" Maria asked.

"Sure. But it wouldn't be easy. The thing that bothers me is there was no other sign of whoever it was," Conner continued. "We can have a better look in the morning. To be sure there is nothing else we can do tonight. The forecast is for a slightly warmer day. I was on with the snow removal guys and they feel it will be another two days before they reach us here. Our train and flights have been rescheduled. There is nothing to do tonight but get some rest."

Each of the group said good night in turn. Maria and Conner left first followed by Jenny and Arianna.

Lucy smiled as she wandered toward the stairs. She sometimes seemed as though she didn't know what to do. She was as much an outcast as Nick. He smiled back wondering if she understood how sad she seemed to be. He still felt that they both had a lot to learn about the real nature of the world.

Nick was the last to head back up to his room. Before doing so, he poured a double scotch from the decanter and finished it off in a single pull.

In the morning, the group gathered at the main entry of the large mansion. The foyer was some twenty feet across and though a large staircase wound its way along the wall opposite the double door entry, there was ample room for the group and several of the household to prepare for the search.

There was a general feeling of concern over what might be someone lost in the snow. A team of hunting dogs had been brought around from the kennel to aid in the effort.

With nearly twenty people, the search party divided into four teams of five. One team would look from the end of the track to the north. Another would check the track going south. The final two teams were assigned to look along the edge of the moor for signs of passage both toward the house and out into the moor itself.

After nearly an hour of searching, a second track was found heading off to the west into the moor. Though there didn't seem to be a connection between the tracks, it was the only other sign of passing and the general feeling was it should be investigated.

This too ended after some several hundred yards. Again, the groups separated to look for other signs of passage.

Again, another track was found heading even further afield.

The general direction of travel was west toward a stand of trees which topped a hill about two miles in the distance. The feeling was that whoever had been crossing the moor was either headed there or had come from there.

The group fanned out searching for clues to the person who'd made the track. By now it had become clear that the track they were now following was fresher than those nearer to the house.

The hill was nearly perfectly round and bore that name by local residences. Round hill. The dome had once been topped by an abbey which now stood in ruin. A fire fanned by desperate winds had destroyed the hilltop edifice two hundred years ago. Though the hill was in the protected lands governed by the Nordhamshin's, no new building had been raised there owing to the violent winds which made the place difficult to enjoy.

The current track led up toward the broken walls of the abbey. One by one the group followed up.

As they climbed, the winds increased. In a short while, they found they had to yell to communicate. After another hundred feet, even that was denied by the deafening gusts.

Nick had taken the lead. As he topped the hill, he found himself facing a long-wrecked wall which had once wrapped the outer edge of the hilltop. Though still impressive, it was toppled in many places. Once it had been a proud wall of nearly ten feet. Now only scant sections indicated its original splendor.

The track pressed through an opening in the wall to Nick's left. He moved toward it and peered through into the courtyard to find the track crossing next to a wrecked stone church. From here Nick could see the beams of the room had fallen through. The building was a skeleton. Where ornate windows had once stood, now were gaping holes which seemed like missing teeth in a giant skull.

The irony of the visual was not lost on him. Instead, he trudged onward. The rest of the group following closely behind.

From inside the church Nick could make out the shape of a person. He seemed to be walking back and forth across the floor searching for something.

Soon it became clear that there was something strange about the man in the church. He didn't seem to be wearing enough clothing to maintain warmth. His frame was almost skeletal. He seemed to be holding a large bundle wrapped in heavy canvas.

The man realized that he'd been discovered.  Suddenly he dropped his burden and looked up at Nick, glaring through his ashen white features.  The lifeless eyes held hatred and malice.

Nick shuddered then moved forward to further investigate the creature he had discovered.  As he advanced, the man seemed to become younger and more vital.  It was only then Nick knew what it was that he faced.

# Togogura Clan

*3 years ago*

The apartment was on the top floor of a well maintained residential tower in downtown San Francisco. They'd been referred to the local contingent of the Togogura family. He was obviously well off and though somewhat secretive about his family connections, it was rumored his family was involved in criminal activity.

After a couple of abortive attempts to connect, he'd finally invited them to his home. This seemed to be something of a formal request as he'd sent a letter on very expensive letterhead to the home of Chun and family.

The Togogura family obviously considered them to be an inferior family. It seemed to be a distinction between nobles and laborers, not racial. Jamas' friends were a working class family that ran a restaurant and martial arts school. The Togogura clan was above menial things.

He'd invited the siblings in after a formal yet simple introduction. It seemed he was impressed with the bearing of the twins. They gave off the feeling of nobility which allowed him a certain comfort. After several minutes of banter, Jamas asked him about the Wight.

"I am told your family has knowledge of a creature that in English is something like a vampire. Our friend called it a Jiangshi. I'm told that there is something similar in

Japanese myth?" Her question hung for a moment. He didn't answer.

"I wondered if you could please tell us what you know of such things," she asked.

"We are researching the legends of these creatures from all over the world. It would make our work easier if you could help."

"You are here because you know. Please, I'm sorry. I understand that there must be some caution on your part. You wouldn't want to seem strange to others. There is no need to worry about that with me," their host stated. "Knowing that you were referred to me by Chun and his kind, I am aware that you know of the darkness in the world. So tell me instead why you have really come."

His manner was direct and almost patronizing, like a parent who'd caught his children in a lie. He showed no anger. He simply stated the obvious transgression and asked for the truth.

"I came across a man who fed on the life of another. I tried to stop him but failed. If I'd had better knowledge of what he was and how to stop him I might have been successful. After following him here to America, I looked up my old teacher hoping he could shed some light on the thing. He referred me to you," she said.

"I see. The old teacher could not give you what you wanted so you came to me. It is not like him to admit he is incapable of facing this thing. Oddly, he and my father once tracked down one of these things together. I would have thought he could give you all the help you might need." The scorn in Injiro's voice was palpable.

"Not to worry. I know he is old. Perhaps I should tell you that he let my father down and was unable to defeat the creature. My father died and made the right choice. He went on to join the light. Your friend told me of his failure and though I don't blame him, I know him to be of lower blood. It was no wonder that he could not kill the thing."

"I'm sorry for your loss," Kayle offered. "But we cannot help the past. We can only affect the future. All we ask is your help in learning how to combat this thing. How do we find it and kill it?" His tone was strong and forceful. He intended to show that he and Jamas were of equal standing.

"Sit," he offered. They moved into the large living area and settled on either of the two chairs which stood opposite of the sofa.

There was no TV in evidence and the decoration was sparse. On side tables along two of the walls were stands containing ten distinctive swords of varying length. All but two were Japanese in design. The others were a French rapier with a very elaborate hilt and a

European longsword which was probably no newer than the third crusade.

Injiro Togogura sat in the low contemporary sofa across from Jamas and Kayle. His apartment was decorated in a style that seemed thirty years too old. Though young and vital, he dressed in complete union with the time gone by.

His black slacks were high waisted and slightly shorter than would be accepted for modern style. They were cut to accentuate his thin frame. He wore a black jacket with short tails that buttoned to a high collar and was similarly cut thin. All that was missing was a white tab and he might be mistaken for a priest. His lean features indicated a man in the height of his physical prowess. Kayle and Jamas could see that he was confident and sure of both movement and thought.

This confirmed their original assessment that he was a martial artist of some skill. From the way he moved, they both thought his styles must be of the traditional Japanese.

Again, he looked them over. His eyes seemed to wander up and down as though taking in every detail in an exact and calculating way. He leaned forward and began.

"There are stories of ghosts that wander the forests of Japan waiting for an unwary wanderer to feed upon. These spirits drain the vital energy from the victim. With each feeding they revitalize their life force and become more and more human again. It is said that if they drain enough living energy they can even recreate their decayed bodies and live again. If this happens they become an ever-living blight upon humanity. Always feeding. Always hungry."

"A creature as this might take centuries to regain its physical form. hundreds of deaths would be the result of its insatiable desire for life."

"The stories say that a person who was wrongly killed or who seeks vengeance for a wrong might become a wandering spirit if their will is strong enough, or if their anger is powerful. Once they begin feeding, everyone who dies by their touch will have a choice. They must either feed or die and return to oblivion."

"Knowing what you will become usually makes this an easier choice than many would think. Faced with an eternity of evil and malice, most chose to pass beyond. A few who desire the illusion of life over the evil that they become chose to feed. They must wander alone in the dark places waiting for their chance to feed."

He smiled as he related the legend. Telling the story of the forest ghost seemed rehearsed for him, as though he'd told it many times before.

"Kyonshi myths were of course an import from China. In Japanese tradition, another name is Gaki. These are spirits which have a hunger for living spirits. It is said that the first of them came from the west. Maybe through China from India. Each has a terrible desire to feed. The earliest were thought to be vampires or ghouls. In every case, they draw living energy through consuming some part of a person as they die. Either blood or flesh will do. Some even feed on the heart torn from the victim while it still beats, or the brain freshly removed from the body."

Jamas and Kayle had been surprised by their host's quick and willing conversation. They'd feared he would turn them away without offering anything they could use. It seemed that he might when they'd first met him but after he looked them over carefully he decided to accept them into his apartment and offer any aid they needed. He described them as peers in a fight to regain his family honor.

"My own trouble began six centuries ago. An ancestor was attacked by a creature and died. A year later he was seen walking in the forest near the family home. It was thought he had become a Gaki. When children and old people began to die without any explanation, the family knew that he had embraced evil."

"Over the centuries since we have formed a secret family society to track down and destroy our ancestor and any who he infects," he paused. "It is an infection in a way."

"Though there is no virus or bacteria, it spreads like a disease. Once drained of life force, a person dies. More and more these people chose to live again instead of following the natural order. I have come to believe that it is because humanity is failing. The good that men do is less than the evil. An imbalance between the two halves of the spirit result in the choice being made to live."

"We all have a hunger, you see. We all desire too much. It is our inability to control these hungers that leads to the growth of evil. People make choices. My family is dedicated to slowing the evil, stopping it if we can. First and foremost, we are dedicated to ending the terror that our ancestor has caused and returning honor to our name."

"The monster I almost caught could have been a Japanese man," Jamas interrupted. "I don't know if it was your ancestor, but it could have been."

"It had been rumored that the head of a large tech company in Tokyo might have been the one. Many of my relatives in Japan have been keeping an eye on him. He disappeared recently and, though the company has continued to operate normally, the CEO has been out of sight for some time now," Injiro replied.

"The truth is we have lost count of his victims. Lately there seem to be an increased need to feed. It is as though his hunger has grown with time. Or maybe with each feeding he desires more. The result is that we have lost track of him as well. Before the war, we knew he was hiding in the court of the Emperor. Since then he has managed to erase all traces. I believe he has the power to change his appearance."

"Of course, there are legends that a Giri can appear as anyone it wishes. I wonder if these powers might require more death to fuel them. So, the insatiable become more insatiable. The hunger becomes uncontrollable. The monster will be revealed," he smiled a wicked smile. "We will discover where he is. We will finish the task in my lifetime."

"What can we do to help?" Kayle asked.

Though the family vocation was nominally related to the rift that they guarded in the cellar of their home, everyone in the family was comfortable knowing there were other battles needing to be faced. Generations of Draksons had dedicated themselves to this secret war.

Injiro paused and leaned back. His eyes moved back and forth between the two siblings as though searching each to determine some unknown truth about them. After a moment, he settled forward again and said.

"We are all in this together. It is not what I need you to do so much as what you know must be done. Continue to track this thing down. If you find it and can destroy it then do so. If you find you need help, simply call me and I will do my best to get to you. My family is rather large.

Like you we have allies everywhere.  Honor is served no matter who destroys the Giri.  Our task is him and his victims who have changed.  All must be destroyed."

"The only information we have so far is that he seems to hunt in nightclubs.  Or did anyway.  If he is the one you seek, he would be smart enough to alter his tactics if he knows he's been found out.  If he isn't the one perhaps he knows where to find your ancestor.  Do you think he would employ his own victims in a sort of clan of Giri?" Jamas asked.

"I will tell you that I have thought it might be so.  My great grandfather had the creature cornered before the war.  He failed because he failed to account for a recent victim who helped the Giri.  Though my grandfather lived to tell the story, he warned us not to underestimate the power that the creature had.  It is said that he can control the minds of a potential victim to instill terror or to force them to his will.  If this power extends to those creatures after their choice then he could have thousands of Giri followers who, though not as powerful as he, could do his bidding."

"The thought is both revealing and frightening.  If these creatures are banding together for mutual benefit, destroying them might be harder than we could hope," Injiro frowned.  "We shall see."

He offered them his personal phone number and instructed them to call should they find any clues.  If they needed any help he would do his best to aid them.  His final words were to be cautious.  Sharing information was the best way to guarantee success.

# The Chapel
*Now*

Nick felt a chill run down his spine as he gazed across the broken church. The eyes that had been hollowed out orbits a few moments ago, were now a deep blue, alive with vitality. The creature had the form of an Englishman in his late forties. The brown hair was speckled with gray. Though still somewhat gaunt, it appeared normal except for the nefarious grin that creased his face.

It was clear that the large bundle the creature had been carrying was a child upon who he had recently fed. The bundle moved occasionally indicating that the child was still alive. From everything that Nick knew, it would soon die and become a ghoulish creature itself.

Nick was unarmed. Still, he rushed the creature and attempted to engage it. Perhaps the child could be saved after all. Maria might have some spell or another to reverse the effects of the infection.

The creature was faster than it appeared, easily sidestepping the rush, and swept its hands down in an attempt to throw Nick to the ground. Nick was not fooled by the move and slipped sideways while throwing a round kick at the thing's left leg which was extended.

The kick impacted solidly just below the knee, snapping the tibia in the process. The creature howled and fell forward as Nick reached for its head with both hands. He grasped at it and pulled it into a choke-out. The iron bands of muscles in his arms began to contract against the blood vessels and windpipe.

Had the thing been living, it would have been unconscious quickly. Instead, it clawed at Nick's arms as it attempted to free itself from his unforgiving embrace.

By now many of the other searchers had climbed into the ruined church. Conner stayed back only a few yards, allowing Nick to do his work. The others stayed back somewhat further in avoidance of the fear generated by the creature.

One of the villagers called out. "Blor' if it ain' Mr. Timmons. And he's been dead on two days now."

"Was an animal attack that's killed him," another cried out. "I was at his funeral."

A murmur of fear ran through them as they talked in low voices saying things about the devil and vampires. One offered Nick a cross as he continued to struggle with the creature. He reached toward him but was so far away that he could not pass the silver object. His fear kept him from going closer.

Nick felt the fear too. It crept into him and caused him to startle somewhat. He'd known fear for long enough to be resistant to its effects. Instead of running or being paralyzed by it, his fear called him to action. He knew that fear would not benefit him in his fight against the thing. He felt it. But he also ignored it.

Conner waited for a moment before reaching for the canvas bag. He pulled the end open, releasing the terrified youth. A large bloody bite marked the boy's forearm. Otherwise there was no evidence of injury. It seemed he might live if he could get proper medical and magical attention. He was immediately identified as one of the townsfolk. His name was Sam.

Nick seemed to be holding his own against the creature but he couldn't change position for a better immobilizing hold. Instead, he rolled back onto his haunches and then to a sitting position. Finally, he wrapped his legs around the thing in a rear mount. Once in that position, he leaned back as hard as he could in order to expose its chest and abdomen to Conner. As he pulled back, he shouted for Conner to "Gut this fish."

Conner stepped away from the shivering boy and picked up a large branch piece of broken wood from the ground. The remains of a pew perhaps. Without hesitation, he stepped forward and pushed the sharper end of the wood upwards into the belly of the beast just below the xiphoid.

The creature shook aggressively as it tried to avoid the strike and free itself from its enemies. Thrashing wildly, it finally tore away from Nick's grasp and rolled to the right onto its hands and knees.

It grabbed at the makeshift spear. With a rapid motion, it pulled out the weapon. In doing so, it also opened a large rip, spilling out its entrails. Then it sank to the ground and twitched several times before falling motionless.

One of the townsfolk retched and fell to his knees. Another crossed himself. Nick climbed to his feet and put his hand on Conner's shoulder. "We need to get the boy to Maria. If what we have been told is true he might end up changing into one of those things."

Nick offered to stay and burn the creature. It was assumed that he was something like a vampire and one of the locals remembered burning was a proper means of destroying one.

Conner stopped to wrap the bite in the boy's arm and ask if he was ok. The boy said nothing. His gaze was fixed and though otherwise uninjured, he seemed to be in shock.

The group trudged back through the snow to the Nordhamshin estate. Conner carried the boy, who was in his early teens.

Nick gathered several shards of wood from the broken benches and pews and piled them in a pyramid over the body of the creature. He used one of the bench ends, which were made of iron, to shave a large bundle of kindling form another hunk of wood. All he needed was a method of lighting it.

After searching for several more minutes, he found a large flat piece of flint near the rear of the church. It was about the shape of the flat stones which formed the façade of a fire pit. He tested the iron on it and found it made a decent spark.

In many of these older buildings, one or more of the flagstones or bricks making the fireplace would have been made of flint.

He struck the flint to iron several times before he got the shavings to smoke. Then, careful blowing caused the fire to begin in earnest. He waited several minutes to make sure the fire would consume the body.

The blaze became a bonfire.

He turned his back on the chapel and followed his companions back toward the house. It would be an hour or more of walking across the frozen marsh to get to the warmth of the house. He pulled the collar of his jacket up and increased his pace.

By the time he reached the estate, Maria had begun working on a spell to relieve the boy from potential infection. She confirmed that he seemed to be carrying a form of corruption.  The family spell she used showed her a red hazed glow which was beginning to take over the child.

She called home and instructed James, the family retainer to check into several journals for anything that might help.  He'd called back within an hour with instructions for separating the corrupting influence from the boy by using a spell that had been recorded in Jamas' journal from her last trip to Asia.

With that much information, Maria was able to build her own version of the spell quickly and administer it to Sam.  His arm had been properly stitched up and he was currently recovering in one of the upstairs bedrooms.

Their worst fears had been confirmed.  Whatever the creature was, it had obviously been created only a couple of days ago.  The group had been staying at the estate for only four days.  Was there a connection?

Nick brought up the point over a large mug of tea.  As the steam rose, he drew in a draft of it through his nose, enjoying the aroma.  "You think that whatever the thing we are after is, it knows we are here in England and set a trap for us?"

"I think it's possible," Conner replied.  "I hate to think I'm paranoid about this but, I wonder if we aren't playing into the thng's hands somehow?"

"What do you mean?" Lucy interjected. "Do you think that the Wight knows we have the skull and is trying to get it back?"

"Yes," Nick interjected. "The more we learn about this guy, the more it seems like he is thinking on a line a little higher than simply eating people for life. I feel stupid to say this but his actions are more human than animal. If this guy's been at it for a while, we might be dealing with someone with a real plan of action. So here is my take: he hides this skull in Africa with someone he thinks he can trust. The obvious reason would be he thinks it poses a danger to his continued existence. That's the obvious reason. What if he let word slip out about the skull in order to trap us. Maybe not us," he paused. "To get someone from the outside involved in whatever his plan is. He needed a catalyst for something. We might have provided the very thing the Wight wanted."

"Which is?" Maria asked.

"I don't know," Nick shook his head. "But I have the feeling we have been played all along. Where exactly did you say you heard about this skull to begin with?" He asked Jenny.

"I am quite well versed in the history and cultures of Asia minor. There had been legends of a monster that was a sort of vampire-like thing going back several centuries in time. I read over some of the magisterial cases from some five or six hundred years in the area. Yes, indeed there were thousands of them and I happened upon the one that I told you about. I've held my post at the university for six years now, and though I'm young for a professorship, I am accomplished," she interrupted herself.

"The records I had been looking though were actually from Miletus but I found that someone had misplaced the Constantinople reports and filed them in the volume I was reading. These volumes are collections of loose vellum which was the writing surface of the time. These had been digitally stored for researchers like myself some ten years ago. Basically, they were all photographed and catalogued. The photo record I was looking through had the one I mentioned misfiled in it. It caught my interest because I remembered having read about the theft of the mystery skull," she continued.

"After verifying my research, I let Keith know." She still called him Keith. "I also learned about the compound where it was being kept and the man who seemed to have possession of it."

"It was on a longshot that we decided Nick should go after it," Conner/Keith replied. "We know all this. What are you playing at?" he asked Nick.

"Don't you feel like you've been setup?" Nick's question hung in the air.

"Now that you mention it," Conner agreed. "I do."

"Here is my point," Nick interjected before Conner could continue. "This thing has been wandering around for centuries. Who knows how long? It can be patient, waiting for whatever it wants. It can lay its plans knowing that time is on its side. Could it be that the skull was taken a decade ago as a step in some long-term plan which it has?"

"I fear that you could be right. But how would we know?" Maria asked.

"I was thinking," Maria continued. "We have been thinking of this creature as a sort of dirty secret. Like a man chasing prostitutes in dark alleys. We have thought of him as a degenerate without any real control over his affliction. In a way, maybe like someone addicted to drugs. He had to get his feeding and would sell his soul to get it. But maybe that's not what he is. Maybe he is more like a predator. He stalks his meal carefully, taking advantage of each opportunity. But, he also is still controlled by a very intelligent purpose."

"It could be that it intends to secure a permanent situation where it can maintain secrecy and security. By offering the promise of eternal life to those who might serve it. It can remain in the shadows and control events. A 'small time' version of the powers we have already overcome."

"If what you propose is true, then it follows that this creature has already been working from that perspective

124

and we are simply touching the very edges of its real plan. What if the thing we fought today was a sort of distraction? Maybe an offering of its lowest level of follower. If it had been made in the last few days, since we have been here, it could be some kind of warning, meant just for us. A kind of 'careful where you tread.' I think we should be careful." Conner argued.

"If that is the case, then we have another thing to consider. It knows we are hunting it, or has planned for us to hunt it, which means we should think about what its intentions are. Why would it want us involved?" Nick replied. Nick had always been the voice of caution. Now that the conversation drifted in the direction of speculation he reverted to type.

"That's some pretty far speculation," Arianna interrupted.

"Perhaps. It's worth consideration though," Conner backed Nick.

"After all we have been through together I would say that there is no such thing as small time. Evil can come in any form. We must be prepared to meet it at face value. Taking for granted that we have overcome a greater enemy might lead us to the mistake of assuming ourselves up to any challenge. This thing might be from our world but as we have already seen, the power of the human spirit is quite potent. This creature might be just as powerful as any we have faced," Maria cautioned.

*Figure 5 Kayles rapier*

# Kayle's Sword

*3 years ago*

The weapon which had become known simply as "Kayle's Sword" was created in antiquity. The general shape of the blade indicated it might have been fashioned in the late renaissance. The hilt seemed to be from a newer age.

Kayle inherited it from his father who had in turn inherited it from his father. The long line going back showed the blade was first recorded in the family history in the late eighteenth century.

Kayle had made an exhaustive study of its origins and the writings on the blade. The Devanāgarī Sanskrit spells of separation, which had been inlayed into the blade, were of a softer metal than the crucible forged steel which comprised the majority of it. The wood scabbard repeated the same set of spells that were inlaid into the blade, these were oak set in maple.

He'd also added the translated spells to the family journals. These had become standard components in much of the family practice since.

The true origin of the blade might have surprised Kayle had he been able to uncover it. Clouded in a mysterious past, he had been unable to uncover its history before coming into the possession of the Drakson family.

In 1789 a certain Italian fencer had ordered the blade's creation. He'd required that no other marks be placed on the blade other than the inlaid writing which only he seemed to be able to understand.

The delicate work had taken nearly a year to complete. Originally the blade was nearly thirty inches in length. The spells had been written only on the first twelve inches below the hilt. A complex basket of silver and steel encased the hilt and a heavy hexagonal pommel ended the weapon with a half inch spike for close fighting.

Ten years later the owner of the rapier returned to the blade smith and asked for it to be repaired. The blade had been broken at twenty inches and the basket hilt had been crushed. Without asking for an explanation, the blade was sharpened with a tapered point just ahead of the break and a simpler cross hilt had been constructed.

The Sanskrit writing was intact and the owner seemed to believe that was the only important aspect of the blade.

Over the years, a legend had formed that the blade had been used to battle an ancient evil creature. It was said that the broken shard remained in the chest of the defeated creature. The hilt had been smashed as a result of the fight.

The fencer had immigrated to the United States shortly after that. It was here that he became employed by the Drakson family, originally as a sort of freelance troubleshooter, later as a butler. He offered his sword to the head of the family as a sign of his devotion.

His name was Giacomo Ambulini. Later he changed it to James Amblin. There had been a decedent of his line in service to the Draksons ever since. It was never said why he came into their service or what caused such dedication. The family had always accepted that James would be there to take care of whatever needed doing.

Kayle had never heard these legends from the family. They'd fallen from attachment to the blade by the time his family had come into possession of it. Even Kayle's grandfather, who seemed to know everything, had not offered more than a hint about its origin.

Through extensive effort, he tracked down the blade maker and learned the true story of its creation.

Giacomo was a tall man. His dark hair and thin features gave him an aristocratic caste. Though not of noble birth, he was from a family of some means. His father had been a merchant. Through trade with the east, he'd built a decent fortune for his eight children to inherit. The oldest brother had taken over the business when the father passed away. The second oldest was promised to the church as was tradition. Giacomo was the third son. He inherited enough to pay for his apprenticeship in

Constantinople as a fencer. He left his family at the age of twelve to study.

During his years there he'd uncovered an ancient secret. A society of men and women who did unspeakable horrors had terrorized the city for centuries. They were known as Sárka Trógon. The family he studied under had begun organizing against the group. He had drawn them into a feud and they aided him in the conflict.

The story was that his friends had been killed by their enemies and Giacomo escaped with only his life and a handful of gold filings. He used these to purchase the weapon he intended for use against Sárka Trógon.

When Giacomo picked up the rapier, he paid using the gold filings. These he claimed to have gotten from a crypt in the old city of Constantinople.

Kayle kept the sword close. It seemed to be a part of him. He'd been given the blade by his grandfather when he reached his fourteenth birthday. Over the next several months he'd been instructed in a very particular style of fencing using the shortened rapier.

Normally the slash and stab stylings of rapier fighting were done using long movements to take advantage of the length of the blade. There had been a school of fighting developed using a shorter dagger of about twelve inches in length which relied more upon quick twisting movements in conjunction with long thrusts.

The form he'd been instructed in incorporated several elements of both. Using the wrist to twist defensively, then slashing in short quick motions, allowed the user to take advantage of a shorter weapon like a dagger while offering the ability to slip into an attack by a longer blade. This would negate a long rapier's advantage and allow quick attacks of both slashing and thrusting nature.

The skill required to use the blade was difficult to learn. Kayle spent much of his spare time working through the techniques that had been passed down through the family. His skill with a normal fencing blade also benefited from this study.

Though he was a heavily muscled person, his grace and skill with the blade had earned him a reputation as a potential Olympic fencer. He considered trying out for the team but decided against it. The demands of both family and study offered no opportunity to take up the challenge.

Kayle and Jamas sat in the pickup waiting. They'd seen the man they were after enter the building some time before and waited for him to return to the car which was parked on the opposite side of the street.

The building was an older twelve story affair with a white stone façade and features reminiscent of the prohibition. The arc top windows had six paned sections below and a radius of petal shaped glass above. Many of these looked original to the building and would have been difficult to reproduce cheaply, which accounted for several that seemed unmatched. These had probably been replacements for ones damaged in one of the several earthquakes that had occurred since the structure had been erected.

Though the sun was up, it hid behind a layer of clouds that often promised but rarely delivered, rain. The drought had become worse with each year and recently the state had issued water saving measures to reduce the unnecessary use of the precious lifegiving resource.

Many round planters had been left to wither and now stood empty along the sidewalk. A few had been converted to trashcans and now overflowed with refuse.

Kayle took another sip from his water bottle. He looked across toward the car and patiently waited. He could feel his sister tremble with anticipation. She was not as patient as he.

"Relax. We have all day. He'll come out soon," Kayle offered.

"Yeah," she replied. "Yeah."

Again, they fell into silence. Her fingers drummed on the dash creating a staccato which reflected her continued emotional state.

Kayle knew there would be no way to get her to relax. When she was itching for action she could be almost frantic. This was simply her way of preparing. She would be ready and calm as soon as any action began. All the energy she built up could then be channeled into the fray to come.

"Look. There he is," she almost yelled.

"I got him," Kayle replied calmly. "He's getting into the car. We'll follow and see where he goes."

"Hurry don't lose him," Jamas whispered trying to control herself.

"Not to worry. I'm on it," he smiled.

The blue sedan pulled away from the curb and drove downward toward the bay. Jamas used her seeing spell and realized he was not infected with the deep red glow of one of the creatures they were seeking. Still he had been the only lead they'd gotten in the last week and they felt it important enough to learn as much about him as they could.

They drove through the city keeping some distance behind to avoid being detected.

Jamas chanted another spell which attached itself to the car so that she could detect it from an even larger distance. She informed Kayle she'd done so and he smiled.

"That's a new one. When did you learn that?"

"I thought it up back in Tokyo. It was barely completed before I found out about Orochi. Turned out it needed some fine tuning so I finished it on the flight back," she smiled.

"Useful," Kayle replied. "What else have you been up to?"

"I have something which might change the way we use our spells completely. Maybe not just on corrupted and evil things but maybe we can affect the world in general. People. Who knows," her voice was filled with the potential of her discovery. She'd been aching to tell him since she'd theorized it, but opportunity and her still unproven technique was not sufficient to give her confidence yet. Once she tested the theory and proved its value, she was certain it could be adopted as a major new weapon in their family vocation.

The man continued on through the city, showing no signs he suspected he was followed. Jamas could see the faint trail of silver thread that represented the effect of her spell. He had a definite destination in mind. He'd gotten on the highway and headed south past the airport. After another hour, they realized he was headed toward San Jose or beyond.

They turned onto Highway 17 and headed out towards the coast. A sign indicated that Santa Cruz was less than twenty miles away. Traffic slowed as they approached the seaside city. Now only five miles of highway separated them from the Pacific.

At an intersection just inside Santa Cruz, he turned southward again. This stretch on Highway 1 seemed to parallel several large estates which formed a high-end community along the beach.

He stopped at one of the more expansive homes and pulled down the drive. There was no place for Jamas and Kayle to park where they could not be seen so they continued onward for another half mile till they found a public beach access and parking lot. They climbed out and headed back along the beach to look for the home. It stood on a rock outcrop which separated the beach they were on with another further up the shore. There was a high tide mark that indicated the next beach was cut off from the one they were on most of the time. Possibly even at the lowest tide.

Though they could see the house from here, there was no way of knowing how long the man might stay without staking out the home from above. Jamas decided to try her seeing spell again and was rewarded with a soft yet deep red glow coming from within the large home. She couldn't make out any other details but she knew that there was a creature in the house.

After checking a map, they found there was a parking area adjacent to a park on the bluff above the house. It would make an excellent place from which to stakeout the estate.

*Figure 6 The Inn on the Moor*

# On the trail

*Now*

It had been assumed that the creature Nick burned was not the only one in the area. Though there had been no evidence of the creature that had created the evil Mr. Timmons monster, he had been known to be alive and normal only a few days before. The natural course of action was to inquire as to his death in a more thorough way.

The magistrate had declared his death accidental by wild animal attack. There had been a natural inclination to assume some kind of rabid or wild dog and an extensive search had been made to no avail.

Maria was not put out by the lack of success. Since she knew that it must have been an undead, she began devising a spell that would hopefully allow her to track or locate any form of undead creature. The spell took several hours to build and once done, she used the method Chris had taught her to enmesh several versions of it into her clothing.

Once completed, she was emotionally and physically exhausted. With the hour being near on midnight she retired to bed. Though she hoped to avoid waking Conner, he stirred when she climbed into bed next to him. Feeling her chill, he snuggled up close to her and offered her whatever warmth he had.

In the morning, Maria and the team went out onto the moor. They went directly to the old chapel on the hill. When they arrived, she said the words that activated one of the spells she'd built and waited for evidence that it had taken hold.

Her vision dimmed, leaving only a thin trail of light which seemed to wander the moor showing the path that the creature had taken. It moved around in a rather unspecific way, as though the thing had been looking for something. Maria began to follow it back the way it came.

She followed it to the place where Nick had seen it during the storm. Then she went along the icy road back toward the town of Nordhamshire. The small hamlet was only another two miles down the road so they simply continued along knowing that they would probably end up there.

Just before reaching the town, Maria stepped off the track and into a graveyard which stood by the town church. She stayed there for a few moments describing to the rest of the team what she saw as a result of the spell.

"It's like the entire world is in twilight except for a swath of about three feet wide. It makes a sort of ribbon of light to form a path for us to follow. There it seems to be moving into the church. As I follow it, it seems to slowly fade as though the longer in the past, the more faint the trail. I doubt I shall be able to follow anything older than four or five days." She seemed concerned.

"I'd hoped to go back to the point where Mr. Timmons had been killed but that may not be possible. Anyway, after the church it follows back toward the constable's office. From there it is very faint. I think it might lead to that house about four down from the inn."

The one she indicated was a stone and wood home like any other in the town though somewhat older. It was constructed of rounded stones mortared together and fitted with rounded beams for roof poles and roofed with modern shingles. The front door was constructed of panels of wood with metal straps that had been hammered at one end into hinges. The other end of the strap formed a classic spade shape.

"I think that would be the Timmons home," Conner offered. I know it's been some great while since I was home but I am sure that he lived there. We went to school together, he, and I. He was a year behind me."

"There is another very faint trail heading out behind the house," Maria said as they moved closer. "I think that is where it starts."

"So he was attacked in his own yard by whatever this thing was?" Arianna asked.

"Yes," Maria replied. "There is also a different kind of trail moving away in that direction." Maria pointed out toward another road which paralleled the main road upon which they'd come into town.

"That road leads to Dellenshire," Conner informed them.

"The new trail seems to be getting stronger so I think we are heading in the direction. The effects of the spell will be gone soon. We've already been walking for over an hour. I think we should arrange some transportation before we continue."

The group walked back to the estate and requisitioned Jenny's car. It would have been uncomfortable for the entire group to climb in so Conner, Maria, Jenny and Nick were chosen. Jenny went along only as it was her car.

When they got back to the Dellenshire road, Maria cast another spell. This one was more selective than the last and would only show the trail of one creature. Maria hoped that its narrower effect would allow for longer activation as Dellenshire was some twenty miles distant.

It took nearly an hour to drive the distance. The road was still slick with ice from the storm. They had also been forced to slow down several times for passing cars due to the narrowness of the road.

By the time they arrived in Dellenshire, Maria was beginning to get tired from the exertion of maintaining the spell for so long. Still, she determined that it ended in an inn which made up the only large structure of the town.

Dellenshire was like many other "towns" in this part of England. It served as a hub for many of the farms which dotted the landscape nearby but was not much more than a gas station and waypoint for travel to any of the larger townships and villages further along.

The inn was owned by the same family for the last two centuries. Their only claim beyond the area was that they had won several awards for their pub ale which was said to be the creamiest that could be had.

By now it was past four in the afternoon and the group felt the need to conclude whatever investigation they could and return to the Nordhamshin estate as darkness would soon make the trip more difficult.

Conner stepped into the inn first followed by Maria and Jenny. Nick came in last. The room was warm and comfortable. Across one side there was a bar behind which a blackboard menu indicated the meals that could ordered. A large open area contained a dozen tables, each with a quartet of chairs. A staircase climbed to what everyone assumed where the rooms for rent.

Behind the bar stood a large man who seemed to be overly friendly. His manner was that of a close friend as he nodded and told Conner he could have any table that was free. There were no other patrons present so Conner chose a table near the fire. Before everyone had been seated, the publican followed and asked about drinks. He expressly emphasized the ale.

Conner and Jenny obliged on the ale. Nick requested water and Maria chose a brandy. Conner smiled and said to Nick. "I know you don't follow those Mormon teachings but you still won't drink?"

"Habit I guess. I may not accept the things I was taught as far as the religion goes but there are some things which I think are reasonable," Nick replied.

Nick had been born in a small community in southern Utah. The reformed church to which his family belonged still chose polygamy as a normal practice. Though he did not subscribe to that or any other of the religious traditions, he did believe it was in the best interest of a person to stay fit. He didn't prescribe to "the body is a temple" doctrine, but more "the body is a tool."

Drinks were brought over after only a minute or two. Each of the team members looked over the inn as though the rather mundane but completely anachronistic, décor could tell them something meaningful.

Finally, Maria said in a low voice. "The room is bright. I mean the whole room. I hadn't noticed it before because we came in from outside and I wasn't thinking about it. I am seeing the whole room as though the creature we are looking for had not only been here but has walked every inch of the room."

"I cannot account for that effect unless the thing had actually walked the entire room." She looked alarmed as she whispered.

"What does that mean? That the creature is still here? Or does it mean that this place has become some sort of... sanctuary of evil?" Conner asked.

"I think it is because the place is intrinsically infused with the energy of the creature. It is as though it left something vital about itself here. I don't know how to explain what I'm thinking," Maria puzzled.

"I can think of a reason for it," Nick interjected quietly. "These things used to be human, right?" he asked.

Maria nodded.

"They are imbued with evil energy that is drawn from the living?" he continued.

Again, Maria nodded.

"They must be able to use some form of spells then. They generate fear and create these residual trails that Maria can see using her own spells. We learned not too long ago that people with imagination can create spells. So, they are dead. They are still human."

"The reason most of the followers of Da Ra Cha Ti could not use magic was because they had been possessed or corrupted by the master. Since his power was not one based on creation, they could not use magic with the exception of the wizard in the second world who was free of a possessing mentality," Maria added.

"What are you thinking?" Conner pressed.

"I think we just ordered beers in what amounts to a trap," Nick smiled.

"Maybe we should come back after we've thought it over more. This is a pretty large discovery. Maybe we should formulate a plan and then come back with a little more caution," Jenny seemed to be shaking.

"I feel it too. There is a fear here. Like the mood of a scary movie. It's barely perceivable, but it's there." Nick, who had as much experience with the fear given off by evil creatures as anyone, seemed to be stating the case for all of them.

"Ok." Conner tossed a five pound note on the table. "Let's get home."

"I'm sorry but something seems to have happened to your car," a friendly voice called from behind the counter. "Seems the tires all went flat from the cold."

"Oh. Let's take a look," Conner said as he moved to the door.

The tires were all flat.  With only one small spare, there would be no way of getting back tonight without new tires from Nordhamshire.

Jenny pulled out a mobile phone and spat a curse as she found there was no reception.  The others all had similar difficulty finding a signal.

The publican quickly informed them.  "The phone is not in working order.  You are welcome to stay the night.  We don't have any guests at the moment so all three of our rooms are available,"

"I guess we don't have much choice," Conner said in a sarcastic tone.  The publican didn't seem to notice the innuendo.

"I'll have the wife get them ready," he replied.

"Ok.  A quick plan is in order.  The closest help is some twenty miles away.  In this weather, it would be tough, but Nick and I both could make it by morning.  It was still early evening, and at a slow foot pace, it shouldn't take more than ten hours or so.  I doubt that Maria, or Jenny could do as well.  But we could try.  My bigger concern is that this place might afford a greater danger than Jenny, at least, has been prepared for.  Maria, Nick and I are active combatants against whatever evil we face and therefore are assumed to be up for the challenge," Conner seemed to be making the case for staying.  He'd reasoned that they were here to investigate the wights and put a stop to their plans. His concern over Jenny was simply that she had not been involved with the group till recently.

"I can handle it," Jenny insisted.

"Good girl," Maria smiled. "I'll take care of you. These two are the toughest and smartest. Between the four of us we will all get out of this fine."

"As much as I hate to make any arrangements without consultation," Conner interrupted, "Nick and Jenny should stay in one room together and Maria and I in the other. That way no one will be alone."

Jenny smiled in a shy sort of way and agreed.

"Don't worry," Nick said in a dry and unaffectionate tone. "We'll sleep in shifts. Two on two off. That way we can be alert for anything." When he saw Jenny's smile shift indicating she'd taken offence, he added "It's just that tonight we should be on alert. I'd otherwise, um, well, if things were different, I... darn." He dropped his gaze in embarrassment.

Jenny softened as she realized she'd embarrassed him. She knew at that moment she had been attracted to him. His hard exterior concealed an intelligent and thoughtful man. She found herself wondering what a relationship with him might be like. Would a man so used to hiding his feelings and living in danger be able to engage in a meaningful relationship with her?

The more she thought about it, the more she realized she felt sorry for having potentially offended or embarrassed him. If nothing else, they were friends. Maybe she should do something to soften the impact of her actions.

She reached over and socked him in the shoulder in a friendly way and said, "Ruck up. No worries. I'll watch first. That way you can dream of what might have been."

Nick seemed to show even more embarrassment at her suggestion. She suddenly felt sorry for him. Nothing seemed to be working.

Maria and Conner seemed amused by the mutual embarrassment of their friends. Maria seemed ready to say something but Conner placed his hand on hers and quietly shook his head indicating he thought it best to let them work it out. Maria nodded in understanding.

Nick realized that no matter what happened, it might turn out to be a long night.

# Caught in the act

*3 years ago*

Waiting was wearing on her. Jamas and Kayle sat in the pickup pondering the next move. Kayle cautioned patience while Jamas wanted to storm the home and deal with the creature.

Kayle reminded her that it might not be Orochi. If it turned out to be him then they might think about acting but if not, then they might need to follow the new creature around in the hope of being led to their enemy. The larger problem was that though they'd both fought corrupted creatures, neither had faced anything that seemed alive.

That there might be repercussions to their actions caused Kayla's caution to win the argument. So, they waited and Jamas fretted over the moments of inaction.

The sun had set some hours before but Jamas occasionally activated her spell and was assured that the creature was still in the house.

"If we don't get any activity before tomorrow morning maybe we should sneak in and check things out," Jamas offered.

"Maybe," Kayle agreed. "It is getting a little boring even to me."

"Kayle?" Jamas asked. "What if these things are a new form of corruption we haven't seen before? What if the Master is upping the game?"

"I guess it is possible. There just doesn't seem to be the same sort of organization about this. I mean it feels different. You said yourself that the vision isn't like the one given off by a normal corrupted creature. And, there is the fact that it seems to be acting in its own interest, not as part of a plan for spreading corruption. Most of the victims die and do not chose to become these creatures. I think it's kind of inefficient to spread the evil this way. The other kinds of creatures we know about are only created for short periods of time or through choice before the act of corruption. This creature devours first, and the choice comes later. I don't know, maybe you are right," he didn't seem to be convincing himself of his own argument.

"It brings another question," Jamas offered. "What would happen to the corrupted creatures here if the Master were defeated? Would they all die off or would they be free to act on their own?"

"That is a good question," Kayle jumped in. "I'd say they might be able to act on their own interest. If they have their own interest, anyway. They are somewhat cutoff from the Master in our world. They might not even realize they'd lost and keep trying to bring corruption through. The dead ones would simply keep operating till they rotted away and were unable to act anymore. The living creatures..." Kayle trailed off, shrugging his shoulders.

"It is really only an academic conversation for now. As long as we are faced with the rift, then we have to keep working against it and its agents. Once we close the gates to the rift and defeat the Master, we'll find out whether our musing has merit."

They fell silent for another few minutes. Jamas decided to try her spell again. The house still showed a pale but deep red glow. She reported the finding to Kayle.

Kayle let Jamas sleep for a while. After about three, she took over watch and checked for the glow again. By morning both seemed a little tired but were more determined to follow through with whatever action might be needed.

Dawn had broken fully and the sun crept over the mountains to the east. A light spread of high altitude clouds mocked the dry parched earth.

Kayle took a drink from a water bottle to wash down the sandwich he'd quickly eaten. Jamas did the same.

With her mouth still half full, she again urged Kayle into action.

"We should take a look. There is still a glow coming from the house and I think we might not get a better chance than we have now," she said as she presented a smile distorted by the large bulge of food tucked into one cheek.

"Ok," Kayle replied. "We might as well. Let's just do this cautiously. We could go knock on the door and see if someone answers. If so, we make up something about our church wanting a donation for children in Africa or something. If not, we can look for a way in."

"It's a plan," Jamas agreed.

They drove back toward the home and stopped along the circle drive. The approach to the house was clearly visible from within so they began acting the part as they walked the rest of the way to the double entry.

Kayle knocked three times then waited. As he looked around, he found there was a doorbell. With a smile, he decided to try it. Just as he reached for it, the door opened and startled them both.

"Yes?" They recognized the man who stood in the door. They'd followed him here from the city the day before.

"I'm Pastor Kayle and this is my sister Jamas. We are here requesting donations for our mission to Africa. We've begun building a school there to teach children about the wonderful deeds that our lord and savior has done in the world."

"Where in Africa?" the man asked. "My recent travels have taken me there. On business."

"Sudan," Kayle offered quickly. "It's a troubled region. The lord's good work might save some."

"I was in south Sudan actually. Business is a little harder there lately. I know the right people though. It's just that I can't imagine a person like you missioning anywhere," the man seemed to be suspicious.

"Well, nonetheless, I'm asking for your help," Kayle pressed. "You see we are having problems of all kinds. Water shortages, no power, food and medicine in high demand. Then there is the simple cost of transporting all the aid to the country. The school doubles as a sanctuary from the violence all around. It is very tough on the regular people. I am just trying to show them the way to the light."

"I'm sorry I can't help. You see I'm not a believer. I've seen many and I can tell you have faith. But I'm not convinced you would do any good there. Most of the people in the world just want to be left alone," he replied. "And your sister seems too violent a person to serve any god. Unless that god you work for is a vengeful one. Oh, but if you are who I think you are, then your god is a very vengeful one," he smirked. "Good day to you," he finished and closed the door.

Jamas fumed silently as they walked back to the pickup. "Tonight," she said as she buckled herself into the passenger seat.

"Tonight," Kayle replied.

They drove toward the town at the bottom of the cliff side. There they spent the remaining part of the day planning their foray. Kayle still advised caution. He pointed out that they would be committing a crime by breaking in. It might be possible that one or more normal people could be injured during their activity.

Jamas pledged to be quiet and patient. Their goal for the night was to discover if the creature they were after was hiding in the house. If so, they would decide then and there what the next step was to be. She reminded Kayle that there was some evil creature of a similar nature to the thing they had been tracking in the house. No matter what else, the thing needed to be stopped.

Kayle knew not to argue about it with her. She would win because he knew she was right. He simply wanted to make sure they would leave no clues as to who they were. He liked his freedom and knew that the general run of the mill police has no idea of the battle between good and evil in the world.

There might be no way to avoid confrontation. It was the duty of the family to fight it in any form it might take. Tonight, he might end up giving his life or his freedom for that duty but it only reminded him of the kind of person he wanted to be.

He and Jamas had fought other creatures of corruption before. Each time the thing had been a corrupted dead. These seemed to be the primary weapon the Master had at his disposal in our world. Each time they had been harder to defeat than before. It would not be long before they might come across an enemy they could not face. Till then Kayle would do what he had to.

They waited till nightfall before returning to the house.

In what amounted to the strangest of coincidences, they arrived just as a car was pulling into the drive. Kayle and Jamas stole silently to the back of the car. They both wore something of a traditional ninja style outfit. Only Kayle brought a sword though.

Two people exited the car and walked calmly to the door. Instead of ringing the bell, one simply opened it and waved his hand for the other to enter. Kayle could tell the other was a woman.

The man seemed tall and thin. His voice pitched slightly high as he asked the woman to enter. She smiled at the obvious false chivalry and walked quickly in.

Jamas grunted at the display and quickly rounded the rear of the car and stole toward the side of the house.

Kayle waited till she was in position before he joined her.

"Let's look around first.  Check all the ground floor windows and see what there is to see.  Then we meet back here and decide what comes next.  If either one of us gets into trouble simply holler. The other will come running.  Recon for now, ok?" Jamas told her brother as though he were the one likely to charge in.

He smiled and nodded his head before rounding toward the back of the house.

Jamas slipped back toward the front, checking in each window as she went.  She stayed below the sill as she moved then peeked up slowly at each.  The first set of windows opened into the large formal living room.  A circular sunken section held a large rounded couch and a center table of oak which sat low to the floor.  Otherwise, the room was empty.

Kayle checked into the first windows he came along and found them to be frosted glass set high in the wall.  This was probably a bathroom.  The second set of windows were much larger.  They let in off the kitchen and dining areas.  Three people stood around a large island stovetop.  The two visitors and an Asian man of medium height.  He seemed to be in his late fifties and somewhat infirmed.  He leaned on a heavy cane of dark wood with a chrome curved handle.  Kayle knew in an instant that the Asian was Orochi.

As he watched, the woman seemed to start.  Her eyes shot open in fear but she seemed paralyzed.  She looked at the Asian man in horror as he stepped closer to her. The other man smiled a wicked smile and moved back a few steps.

Kayle looked around for some clue as to what he should do. Near him toward the rear of the house was a deck which had a set of sliding doors leading to the kitchen. Without thinking, he rushed toward them and gave a loud shout. "Chúfáng!!!" He knew she would understand the Mandarin for kitchen.

As he tore open the sliding door, the Asian turned his attention quickly to him. Jamas rounded the corner just after and stepped in beside him. They stood side by side, each half facing away from the other.

Jamas took a standard half stance with her hands in a high low. Kayle leaned forward in a modern wrestler's pose, both hands at just above his waist.

Suddenly, a deep fear gripped them both. Kayle could feel the surge of despair course through his body as though pumped by his own heart.

Jamas uttered a word and the fear was blasted away. She stepped forward and told the woman to leave.

She stood there in a dazed, still gripped by whatever controlling force the Asian had over her. Her eyes seemed dazed and without focus. She also seemed to be swaying a little like a tree in a soft summer breeze.

"Wake up!" Jamas yelled at her.

"She is mine," Oroshi said with contempt. "This time you brought someone to help. That is a good idea since I have my own help now."

He waved his hand and ended in a point toward the twins. The man and the woman stepped forward as one in an obvious attempt to shield Oroshi from harm.

Kayle moved forward to engage the man while Jamas stayed in her stance some distance back.

The man stepped forward quickly and stabbed a punch at Kayle's face. Kayle dodged to one side like a boxer and landed two jabs with his left hand directly at the man's jaw. The man staggered back and then fell to the floor unconscious.

Jamas used another of her spells. This one aimed at Oroshi. She hoped that by distracting him with a glamour he would release control of the woman. A glittery shower of light which only Oroshi could see caused him to stagger back. In doing so, he let go of his control of the woman and she screamed a loud terrified shout then ran from the room in terror.

Now the twins faced Oroshi alone.

He stepped forward and seemed to relax. There appeared to be a shadow that covered everything but a small swath around his eyes. The light in the whites of his eyes seemed to almost glow. The dark pupils erupted in an expression of fear.

Jamas had been exposed to this effect before and was prepared for the foreign sensation to hit her. Kayle was emotionally staggered but stood his ground.

The feeling grew in intensity as they both seemed unable to control their bodies. For several seconds, they struggled to fight back the terror which the creature exuded. Only through sheer will power did Kayle break the effect and move a step toward his adversary.

Oroshi had been smiling an evil smile till then. The grimace turned to a frown when he realized that Kayle was no longer bound by the effect of his power. With a quick gesture, Oroshi turned and fled down the hall toward what Kayle knew must be the garage.

As Kayle followed, Jamas was also released from the power of Oroshi's terror. She shook off the feeling of powerlessness and ran to catch up.

Oroshi had just made it to the door and was tugging at the handle when Kayle caught him. Kayle grabbed him by the collar and pulled quickly back. Oroshi was much stronger than he looked. He held tight to the door knob which broke free of the door as the combined strength of the combatants tested its integrity.

Oroshi turned toward Kayle and lifted his leg in a wide arcing crescent. The kick caught Kayle on the side of the head and smashed him against the wall. His grip on Oroshi loosened enough for the wight to escape.

Oroshi dove through the door which now swung open easily. He rolled to his feet in the garage and tore open the door of the sports car which was parked in the center of three spaces. Before Kayle could recover or Jamas could enter the garage, the car's engine sparked to life and Oroshi drove straight through the metal panel door without regard. The crashing of metal against metal and scraping steel rang loud in the late evening air.

Oroshi had escaped again.

# The Inn

*Now*

Nick felt the mist around him. It was heavy and gray. There was a weight to it. It felt as though he were being pressed down against the bed. The sensation was less physical and more a feeling of oppression. A familiar feeling. One he'd battled against many times, in fact. The mist was fear.

Near him, he could hear a scratching sound. It repeated several times then he heard a click followed by a squeaking. It sounded like a door being slowly opened. In the mist, he could see a door framed darkly. Around the rectangle portal there was a halo of black. It was as though everything was in negative colors. The dark grey of the mist and the black inky radiance from the edges of the door.

The door began to swing open. The creaking increased. The blackness began to swallow his vision, blinding him with its power. The blackness was the fear. He awoke.

Nick shot up to a sitting position. The cover fell away as he peered across the room toward the door. He could make out two figures. One small and one much larger. They slowly skulked toward him. He reached a hand to touch Jenny who sat in the chair which had been pulled close to the bed. He felt her shiver in terror.

Nick felt the fear too. It penetrated him like a wave of nausea. He realized then that Jenny was so terrified she was unable to move.

Nick had a momentary loss of motion as well. He'd faced fear enough that it was like an old friend who he hated but knew well enough to drink with. Not that Nick drank. His temporary lapse of control was not natural to him. It bothered him that he could feel the fear so deeply that it might immobilize him.

He also knew that fear could come at any time and, once in a while, even a hardened veteran like himself might succumb to its power. Nick fought it only for a moment then was rewarded with control over the emotions which might have killed him.

Knowing that Jenny might not be able to overcome the feeling, he leapt toward the interlopers. He'd hoped to catch them off guard by his action. The larger of the two intercepted him with an amazing display of reflex.

Though Nick managed to wrap his arms around the attacker, he was unable to move him back. He felt a cold breath close to his face and fell back a step while reaching out to hold off the impending attack.

Nick's eyes had adjusted to the lack of light by then and he could make out his opponents. Each was gaunt and seemed emaciated. The smaller was a woman. The larger a man.

The woman's face was pale and the skin was stretched across her face, pulling back the lips and exposing her jagged teach in a grimace of hatred. Her eyes sunk in their sockets and thin strands of hair whipped back and forth as she moved toward Jenny in a shuffle.

The man was similarly skeletal. Though much larger, he seemed to be a dry husk of a man. What clothes he wore hung on him in tatters. He reached with both hands toward Nick and smiled through an open maw, showing a dried tongue which hung to one side of his mouth.

Nick intercepted both hands, gripping them from below and trying to push them upward to expose the man's abdomen to possible attack. The man resisted. Though thin and seemly brittle, he possessed a great reserve of strength. As Nick struggled against him, the creature seemed to grow even more mummified. His cheeks seemed to hollow out and the eyelids no longer closed as they were stretched tight. Nick seemed unable to push upward so he changed tactics. Pulling his left hand down and to the right, he crossed his arms and simultaneously stepped to the right. He let go with his right hand and quickly wrapped it under the thing's chin. Then, pulling back with all his strength, he was able to force his opponent in front. His left hand shot down below the creature's arm and up again to a half nelson. Once secured, Nick gripped his left elbow with his right hand, creating a choke-out.

With a small hop, he wrapped his legs around the thing's waist, throwing it's weight off center. The thing fell back just as Nick had planned. Though he landed on his buttock with a heavy thud, he was now in the classic rear mount position and in complete control of the encounter.

Again, Nick arched his back and pulled. A soft snapping sound could be heard. The creature let out a grunt then began to resist. Nick flexed his biceps trying to cut off circulation and breath. He held for several seconds but the thing seemed to suffer no ill effect. In only a moment, the thing had come back to a sitting position.

It reached down with its right hand and grabbed Nick's foot. It pulled sharply upward and Nick could feel the ligaments in his knee begin to strain. Quickly he twisted his arms trying to break the creature's neck. It resisted that attempt as well. Nick was forced to let go of his grip and roll to the left to avoid damage to his leg.

While doing so, he sent a parting kick to the creature's head and rolled quickly to a crouching position. He managed to get his hands up in defense before the creature was able to renew its attack.

He risked a glance toward Jenny. She was unmoving. The smaller wight had pinned her to the wall it had not attacked yet. It simply held her in place and stared into her eyes. He could tell that Jenny was terrified beyond any reason. He returned his attention to the larger thing just in time to intercept a swipe to his face.  The creature's fingers had mummified to the point they seemed more claws than human digits.  The attack might have left deep gouges had he not slapped it in passing.  He leaned back far enough for the next swipe to miss him by mere inches.  This attack he checked down while counterattacking with a quick jab to the jaw.

Nick followed up with another check-down and jab with the other hand.  The creature reeled back at the sudden strikes then leaned forward trying to wrap its arms around Nick's chest.  Nick lifted the left elbow of the thing as it stretched forward and sent a strong right hook just below the ribs.  He pulled the arm across and was rewarded with an exposed back.

This time Nick balled his fist and swung heavily at the thing's head.  A loud crack was followed by the creature falling bodily to the floor.  It twitched twice then was still.

Nick didn't wait for the thing to fall.  Instead he turned his attention to the smaller of the two creatures which now menaced Jenny.

In two steps, he was close enough to grip the creature by the neck and lift it straight up.  It seemed to be incredibly light and Nick's motion slammed it against the ceiling.

The thing quickly spun in his grip and wrapped its legs around his neck.  Nick's right arm was trapped in the attack, which turned out to be a good thing. As the creature slowly squeezed, Nick found that his arm was in a position to protect his windpipe from being crushed.

In a desperate move, he jumped upward and swung his arm downward. Putting all his weight in the motion allowed him to slam the attacker to the floor with a heavy crash.

The thing went limp. Nick was able to extricate himself from the skeletal remains. The fear seemed to have vanished. He looked over to Jenny who was sobbing. She sat on the floor under the window with her face in her hands. He crossed to her and gently placed his hands on her should and said. "It's over now. You are ok."

She nodded. Still weeping, she stood up and tried to smile. Then her face went into a frown and she said between sobs. "Conner, Maria."

Maria was on watch when they came. She felt a sudden surge of fear well up in her. She'd felt this artificial fear many times before. She knew it for what it was and whispered a word which activated the spell to override the effect. A small line of Greek characters faded from her sleeve.

The faint scratching followed by a click and squeak heralded the arrival of the enemy.

Three figures filed into the room. They seemed unaware of the fact that Maria felt no fear. She reached out and touched Conner's arm. The reward came when she heard his soft, "Yep."

All three were in the small room now. It felt slightly crowded once they'd flanked out forming a line blocking the door.

Maria wasted no time. With a whisper, she unleashed an unbinding spell. It should have had an area effect but only the center of the three seemed to have been bothered by it. The other two stood tall while it crumpled to dust in only a moment.

The enemy now began to advance. Though slow and measured, they seemed confident in their ability. The first made it to the foot of the bed before Conner was able to kick free of the covers. In a move of masterful agility, he snatched the blanket as it rose and wrapped it around the head of the first of the two. He pulled downward and smashed the creature into the wooden foot board, which splintered at the impact. The creature seemed to be unaffected by the violent maneuver and struggled under the restraining wool.

Maria called on another spell. This one forced the creature back as though blasted by a strong wind. It strained against the unseen force for several seconds before finally taking a step forward. By this time Maria decided on the right attack and blasted it with an ethereal fireball. A large spherical blue light erupted from the creature. The light quickly resolved into an azure inferno. The thing fell to the floor clawing at its face and arms, trying in vain to put out the nonexistent flames.

Conner began to pound at the blanket wherever large protrusions occurred. Once he realized the thing weighed very little, he gripped several handfuls of material and lifted it like a large sack. This he sung over his head and slammed into the floor. The creature still struggled inside the bundle. Conner repeated the move, adding the weight of his motion as he heaved upward then drove down. The bundle still struggled but less than before. Again he lifted and drove it into the floor like some enraged lumberjack.

It twitched a little.

He arced it over his head again. Thump.

Twitch.

Thump.

Twitch.

Thump.

Silence.

"I think you got it," Maria smiled.

"Yeah," He replied between breaths. "You?"

"Yep," she grabbed his hand and smiled.

"These trips are getting to be dangerous," he joked. "Let's go check on Jenny." The fact that he hadn't mentioned Nick was only because he figured Nick could watch out for himself.

They entered the hall at the same time as Nick and Jenny. Each was relieved that the others seemed no worse for wear. The group decided they should investigate the rest of the inn to make sure there were no other potential threats. Conner and Maria wandered through the remainder of the rooms upstairs while Nick and Jenny checked the main floor of the inn.

Other than the four, the inn was abandoned. Time had slipped past four in the morning. After a quick discussion, it was decided restarting the fire in the pub below and spending the rest of the night on rotating watches seemed prudent. This way the team would be stronger should anything happen during the remainder of the night. Nick and Jenny were assigned the first hour, Conner and Maria would try to sleep.

But first they talked to try to quiet Jenny who seemed to have been unsettled by recent events. As they huddled around the fire, they talked about the encounter. Jenny's trouble seemed to be related to her inability to fend off the terror generated by the creatures they'd fought.

"It's not something people face every day. That kind of terror can paralyze even the most seasoned. You have nothing to be ashamed of," Maria calmed her.

"It's not that," Jenny quietly admitted. "Well, not just that. I am not the kind of person who gets hysterical. To lose control like that. To not be able to act. It's just hard for me to take."

"We have all faced these kinds of things before," Conner added. "You mustn't believe anything less of yourself for what happened. Next time you will be better prepared."

"There will be a next time," Maria continued without acknowledging Conner's words. "And there will be a next time. Once exposed to this sort of thing you become something of a magnet for it. I mean to say that by being aware of it, you will discover yourself intrinsically get drawn into the sphere of activity of these things. If you like, I can teach you some things to help. A few spells and how to create them. Over time you might find that you have a natural gift for it. There are, of course, other ways to deal with these things. You could develop skills as a fighter or a researcher."

"Thank you. I would like to feel safe again but now that I know... I just don't know if it is possible. I was aware in an academic sort of way. I never really knew though," Jenny seemed somewhat bolstered by Maria.

"The more you learn, the safer you will be. What we do is full of danger of course, but learning about it and developing skill is the best way to defend yourself," Maria advised.

Though she still seemed uncertain, Jenny smiled hesitantly and replied "I'll try."

The remainder of the night passed without incident. Though none of the four managed to get any sleep, they did discuss the night's attack and decided to do a thorough search of the inn once the morning arrived.

The inn was set up with a public bar, a kitchen, and the main living quarters of the publican and his family on the first floor. The second flood consisted of the guest rooms.

One room in the family apartment had been used as an office. A computer monitor stood in the center of a rather messy desk. On it was a series of text messages between the innkeeper and some unknown person with the Japanese handle "KoraiRojin."

Conner, an expert in Asian culture, translated it to mean dark ancestor or old man. He thought to write it down and get Arianna's take as she was better with languages.

The bulk of the texts revolved around what seemed to be inventories in small quantities. Two of these and one of those. The things which were listed happened to be in Japanese as well and Conner thought they might be animals or children. The symbols used translated to words related to puppies or bear cubs. He felt like there was some form of code worked into it otherwise the lists might have made more sense.

The final few messages indicated that the publican had some guests which he thought might be dangerous to the family. The responding instructions indicated the interlopers should be brought into the family.

I small shiver ran up Nick's back as Conner read the final line. It meant that the events of last night were supposed to change the four of them into these creatures.

He voiced his thought.

"They might have tried but I believe we would not have become like them. It takes a choice. There is always a choice. If you give in to the desire, then you embrace evil. We all are strong and sure of ourselves. We have wills that could resist. It means we would have died," Maria informed him. "You might have died but you would never have become a servant of evil."

"I'm glad of that at least," Conner added. "Can we figure out anything else from the computer or the files in here?" he asked.

The search turned up several correspondences from a patron in Africa. The nation of origin was startling as Nick had been there only a short time ago. It was where he had pilfered the skull. Further notations and files from the computer led Nick to believe that these people had been changed into wights by someone who lived in the compound he'd infiltrated.

*Figure 7 Constantinople*

# Giacomo

*The past*

The tall man seemed to be waiting. His black hair and thin moustache indicated he was high born. His elegant red and green brocaded jacket was meticulously matched to his pantaloons and shoes. From a distance, he might be considered another fop strutting his nobility for the passerby.

The citizens were unimpressed with the man as they were all preoccupied with recent events. Downward looking eyes and somber attitudes gave away the fear and depression that had gripped the news of late.

The market district had the worst of the plague. Bodies of the dead littered the streets and amongst all of that, a darker threat loomed. A few of the dead bodies seemed to have been partially eaten. At first it was believed that rats had managed to get to them after death.

A few learned men had insinuated that the bites were the cause of death. Those few bodies showed no signs of the red mottled sores that were the hallmark of plague.

Giacomo cared little for the worries of the common man. Though young, he was just apprenticed to a master swordsman here in Constantinople. He waited for the carriage that would collect him for the first part of his new adventure.

He'd earned his opportunity by having won several local tournaments. His technique was still considered amateur by the nobles of the world, but for the son of a highly successful merchant, he was of the best.

The difference was in availability of training. Only true nobility could afford the complex training that would make him a master, the highest rank attainable in skill with a rapier. The lowest skill level being adept and the middle level being practitioner. It should be noted that there were a very few who were considered grand masters of fencing.

He studied at a local school after his father died. Being third in the family meant only a small staple for living expenses. He knew that his fortune depended on learning a skill he could market. His particular penchant for the rapier offered the best potential to better his place in society.

He had just passed his eighteenth birthday and was moving to his master study with the Belino family. The patriarch had developed a particular defensive strategy based on non-linear movement. These he claimed to have learned from an Asian aesthetic who he'd met in the warehouse district in the ports of Constantinople. It was because of this technique that Belino was considered a Grand Master, and a new school of practice was developed from his technique.

Mixing these theories with modern practical fencing had formed the basis of a new and highly sought after technique which, when used properly, was said to be undefeatable.

For Giacomo's competitive accomplishments, his rank was said to be near that of a master but he still lacked the subtle and more advanced skills that would graduate him to the highly sought after title. To study with someone with the reputation of Belino would provide him with the necessary prerequisite to be considered a master.

The carriage which stopped in front was drawn by a pair of white and grey horses. They seemed matched in every way. Tall and elegant, each sported gilded tac and harness.

The carriage itself was painted in a red and green motif. Along the edges of the design, gold inlay and metalwork complimented the almost garish motif. Giacomo had chosen his garments for the day to match the colors of the house in which he was apprenticed.

The footman swung down from the rear of the carriage in a practiced and graceful swoop. An overly exaggerated bow to Giacomo was followed by him opening the door and flipping down the carriage step.

Giacomo bowed gracefully and gathered himself into the carriage.

He sat facing the front. The other seat, which faced rear, was occupied by another young man of about the same age. He wore similar clothing with a slightly more affluent gilding. Giacomo introduced himself.

The other occupant replied in kind. His name was Ferdanand De Copa. Giacomo recognized the name as a famous fencer from Spain. It was said he was the nephew of the king of Spain. Giacomo suddenly felt a little embarrassed at being in the company of royalty. Though he had met nobles before, the idea of interacting with them on an equal footing seemed alien.

This feeling was soon put to rest as Ferdinand and Giacomo became fast friends. They'd arrived at the estate of the Belino family and over the next year and a half spent much of their time together.

There were several other students at the estate but Belino spent a great deal of time with the friends. These were paid apprentices and therefore he gave them the benefit of his personal attention.

Every day they'd practice for five hours before being instructed in courtly graces and other gentlemanly pursuits. The two attended banquets and parties on the weekends and were expected to present the perfect image of a student at the Belino school.

Even with all the other diversions, the two found themselves working harder and harder at the sword.

Many evenings, while waiting for the dinner hour, they would discuss what they'd learned that day and fein encounters to hone the skill.

Though Ferdinand was better at close fighting, his technique was very forced and Giacomo found he could sometimes use nontraditional movement to create an opening. Giacomo found his long technique to be superior but Ferdinand could often twist into a long attack and find his mark.

In all other ways, the two were equals. Many days, the entire five hours of conditioning was spent in sparring. There were times that neither managed to touch the other.

After the first six months, the two attended a tournament where they both reached the final. Facing off against each other, they managed to fence for nearly three hours before the judges declared a draw.

In the year that followed, they also became what amounted to family in the Belino household. The patriarch often called them his sons. The other members of the house called them "Daemones Furca" the Devil's Forks.

Balilo had two sons and three daughters. His sons were both younger than ten and often admired Giacomo and Ferdinand. Sometimes the young Belinos pretended to be The Devil's Forks. They would pretend to fight off villains and bandits and offer up their exploits as long stories around the fire after dinner.

Giacomo felt he had found a home better than any he might have known with his own family. By the end of the second year, the Belino family offered him a chance to stay and become a teacher for new apprentices. He accepted without thought.

The following year Ferdinand left for his home in Spain. His father had passed away and he was called back to take up the title of Duke in the small province he called home.

Though Giancomo was saddened by his friend's leaving, he took up his new appointment. Over another years' time he became known as second only to Belino himself.

It was then that his patriarch confided in him a secret. The dark and deep secret of why an Italian family had taken up residence in the outskirts of Constantinople. They were tasked with watching and recording the goings on related to an olive tree in the grove behind the estate.

This one tree was said to house the spirit of the light. No one harvested olives from its limbs. Every Saturday at midnight the patriarch would sit at the base of the tree and look into the knotted trunk at a small band of light which crossed from lower left to upper right at about 75 degrees.

Giacomo was occasionally tasked with the "watch." During these times, he thought he could see into other places in the world. Sometimes he found he could imagine seeing Ferdinand going about his daily life in the stone castle which he called home.

At first the visions he saw frightened him. By the passing of another year, he enjoyed the time he spent watching. Often he would spend the entire night gazing into the crack of light. Belino warned him that he could only watch on Saturdays because of the narcotic effect of spending too much time at the tree.

During his other hours of leisure, Giacomo wandered the ancient streets of the city. He was secure in his ability to defend himself so not even the lower quarters were off limits to his explorations.

His study had left him with an insatiable desire for knowledge. He often found himself at old churches and mosques studying the intricate writings and inscriptions.

His love of Byzantine mosaic caused him to search every quarter of the city for anything which might wet his appetite.

He'd heard of an ancient catacomb which had been the burial place of several saints. In these, it was said, some of the greatest works of early Christian mosaic were to be found.

After some inquiry, he'd managed to find a map of the catacomb in question. With this and a lantern in hand he set out one Saturday morning to discover these masterpieces of art.

Using the map as a guide, he wandered for several hours before he realized the map was wrong. He'd paid four coppers for it and felt cheated. If he managed to find his way out, he'd look up the swindler that had sold him the worthless paper and teach him a lesson.

After a moment of feeling angry and then despondent, he decided there was nothing to do but wander in one direction till he managed to find a way out.

At each intersection, he turned right. Unless he was trapped in a direct rectangle he would either run across his own footsteps or find the way out. In order to know which was true, he brushed away the cobwebs of each corner he passed. If he ran across a clean corner he'd know he was wandering in circles and add one left to his turnings.

After several more hours, he found himself in a large chamber which was nearly twenty feet to a side. The only exits were the way he'd come and another passage on the opposite wall. In the center of the chamber stood a large sarcophagus of stone topped with a statue of a medieval knight laid to rest with his sword in hand lain down the length of his body. The lid had been moved off the stone repository slightly and now stood open enough for Giacomo to look in and discover that the grave was empty.

He raised his lantern and looked around the chamber. Along the walls and across the entire domed ceiling were laid beautiful mosaics of an early style. They seemed to be from the first crusade as they depicted the coming of the peasant army which had been known as the People's Crusade led by Peter the Hermit. It depicted a mass of people being ushered quickly across the Bosporus by the patriarch of Constantinople.

As Giacomo stood inspecting the mosaic, he heard from the opposite passage the sound of scraping footsteps. An unknown fear welled up in him and he felt he should hide from whoever might appear in the passage. Quickly he dowsed his lantern and slid back into the passage he'd recently used.

The sounds of the footsteps came louder and louder. Soon a pale light could be seen slowly progressing down the other passage toward the large chamber.

Giacomo could make out two people. The first was a young woman of lower birth. Her linen dress was slightly stained from whatever work she did. Her face was placid and though there seemed to be a certain emptiness in her eyes, he could see that she was walking of her own volition.

The man who followed her seemed to be old and frail. Though his garments suggested he was of noble means, they seemed outdated and unkempt in a way that Giacomo could not understand.

Once the two entered the chamber, they came to a stop just next to the sarcophagus. The woman turned to the man and extender her arm.

He took the offered appendage and said a word in an old form of Greek. Suddenly the woman seemed to be loosed from her state of passivity. She screamed and began to struggle against the seemingly ancient aggressor.

He held tight to her wrist. An evil smile slowly spread across his face, causing it to seem to wrinkle into a grimace of pure terror. He bared his jagged teeth and brought her arm up to his lips.

She screamed again as his teeth sank into her flesh. Though her entire body struggled, her arm was immobile as the man tore a large patch of skin and muscle from the now exposed bone.

Her body fell to the floor, lifeless.

The man chewed on the raw flesh as blood dripped from his face.

Giacomo was startled to see him change then.

The man's face began to smooth and become youthful. His thin straggly white hair grew think and black. The skin seemed to puff outward and fill with new vitality.

As the transformation completed, the man took in a deep breath. The first, Giacomo realized the man had breathed during the entire time he'd watched. The fear which had radiated from him stopped affecting him.

A feeling of vengeful pride came into the fencer. He should stop this man from the evil he was doing.

But the man was obviously a devil of some kind. He could change his appearance and create fear. How would Giacomo fight such a thing? Perhaps his master would know some way to deal with it. He resolved to follow the thing from the catacomb and report to Belino on his discovery.

The man picked up the body of the woman and wandered back the way he'd come. Giacomo followed as quietly as he could. He tried to keep them in sight but at a few turns on the way he lost them except for the glow coming from...the man had no lantern.

Whatever light followed him was also of unnatural origin. He knew then he must report the man to the church so he could be tried as a witch.

After what seemed another several hours the man stopped at an open grate. He pulled a chain which dangled from the arched overhead and a section of the metal barrier slid upward. Here he dropped the body of the woman and turned back the way he'd come.

Giacomo ducked into a side passage and allowed him to pass before progressing to the exit.

Once free of the catacomb, he wandered back to the city center and found a carriage for hire to take him back to the estate.

The hours he thought had passed during his exploration of the tunnels turned out to be only two. He reasoned that fear and excitement had caused him to think time was running faster than it really had been.

Once home, he told Belino what had transpired. At first he thought his mentor would think he'd gone mad. But then after a long silence, Belino told him the truth.

"We have been watchers of the tree for centuries. Our family came here during the crusades and became famous for our fighting skills. We trained five generations of crusaders and since then fencing has been our livelihood."

"But here on the estate we found that the tree was a connection to the world above. Heaven, if you can call it that. We can see into that world from here. As you have seen through the tree to know what your friend Ferdinand is doing, so can we see events around the world. There are those that would use this power to foretell great disasters and to spy on the just," he paused.

"There are also devils that could use the tree as a gateway to heaven. They might be able to force their way back into the halls of God and do some harm to the hosts of the father. We are tasked to protect this shrine from them as well. I fear you may have found a devil from hell. It is possible that he might use you to get to the tree. We must be vigilant."

Giacomo was nearly unnerved by Belino's revelation. How could he fight creatures of evil? A man could die at the hands of his blade. A devil with no soul may not die as men do.

Giacomo asked the obvious question. "How can we send it back to the fires?"

"There is a way. Faith in the father gives us the strength to battle any evil. But we must meet him in the middle. I'll look into it. For now, continue to do your teaching and I will go to the church and talk to Father Andonito."

Though a loyal Christian, Belino had not shown this level of dedication before. As a noble, the family and its retainers usually attended mass at their private chapel on the grounds of the estate. Father Domiano, who tendered mass at the family chapel was a younger initiate and it seemed that Belino wanted the council of a more experienced clergyman.

"He may have knowledge that can be used to aid us. This is now our task. In a way, you have furthered our family cause. You are as my own sons. I will place you in trust with the protection of our family," Belino smiled.

"I won't disappoint you. I promise to protect our family no matter the cost, be it my own life and soul." Giacomo felt a well of pride at the thought of being accepted as a sort of adopted son.

"Well spoken, my son. Be patient for now. Thank you."

Belino left quickly while Giacomo returned to the fencing yard where he spent several hours going through the complex techniques he'd learned.

Dinnertime saw the family dining without Belino. He had not returned from his impromptu meeting at the church.

As the house settled to bed, a messenger came with word from the rector that Belino was staying overnight in prayer.

The morning arrived with no further word from Belino. Giacomo began to worry and decided he should venture into the city and find his benefactor.

He arrived at the church amid a stir of activity. After inquiring with the rector, he was informed that there had been a death at the church the night before.

Giacomo felt his heart sink thinking that it might have been Belino. When the identity of the deceased was revealed his worst fear was confirmed. The rector told him that Belino left the church just before dark.

"But we received message from you that he was to stay here in prayer?" Giacomo pleaded.

"I sent no such message. Besides, it is only Father Andonito and myself here, we have no one to send as messenger." The rector seemed genuinely concerned. "Perhaps father Andonito can shed some light on this. He was the last to speak to Belino.

The rector escorted Giacomo inside the church and to the rear offices to the right of the alter. They passed through the door and came into a large library which served as the office. At a heavy walnut desk done in a French style sat the priest of the parish.

Giacomo felt sick when he realized he'd seen the priest before. In the catacomb.

The priest stood behind the desk and extended his hand in an obvious attempt to intimidate the visitor.

Giacomo felt a sudden swell of resolution and determination as he forced his hand forward to accept the offered sign of respect. He shook the cold skeletal hand.

Here was the one responsible. He would face him if he could. If Belino had been killed by this man, then he would need to prepare. He would need to be ready for anything. More than that, he would need a weapon against evil. He knew that a simple rapier would not kill a devil.

He stayed and asked after Belino and what had occurred though he didn't bother listening to what the priest had to say. Instead, he wondered what it would take to exact revenge for the death of his mentor.

The return home was interminable. How would he be able to explain to the family he was supposed to protect that their patriarch was dead because of something he himself had discovered?

He felt responsible for the death. Though he told himself over and over again that it was the devil that had killed Belino, he still felt a deep regret.

Upon returning, he went directly to Belino's wife and told her the news. She fell into his arms and wept loudly. She asked that Giacomo tell the news to the children as she could not bear to tell them.

He did, and they cried. Giacomo stood before the two boys and told them that they were the men in the house now. It would be up to them to watch over the business and take care of their mother.

They stood up and wiped their tears. Each put on the face of courage and nodded accent to Giacomo's charge.

Giacomo still faced the same problem: how do you kill a devil? For days, he pondered the problem. When Saturday night came, he started his vigil at the tree with the question still in his mind.

When the light came from the crack in the tree, he saw something he'd never seen before. There was a long silver blade with strange writing along it. He saw the blade kill a monster in the vision.

Sunday after mass, he set out to the swordsmith his family used. There he ordered what would become the famous blade of Giacomo. When he described it in detail and felt the smith had enough information to make it correctly, he asked how long it would take to make.

A blade of silver would require a great deal of time. To make the silver strong enough, the metal would be alloyed with others giving it both strength and flexibility. It would not be as strong as steel but it would otherwise be capable of killing. Forging such a blade and finishing it as directed would take a year.

The price was extremely high. And though he could not afford the amount, he ordered it made anyway. The name of Belino was enough for the smith to start it. Giacomo had one year to come up with the price.

He spent the year practicing and teaching and doing his best to take care of the family he'd somehow inherited. The reputation of Belino was enough to keep new students coming to the estate to train. Giacomo had even developed a reputation of his own as a grand master of the rapier.

As the time approached for him to collect the weapon, he began searching the catacomb for the chamber he'd visited the year before. Though he remembered the general directions, time and anger had blunted his memory of the event.

After several weeks of searching, he finally found the chamber. There in the center was the sarcophagus which he remembered from his earlier visit. The lid still askew and the stone knight still slumbered atop.

As he inspected the chamber, he realized that the sword was gilded in thin layers of gold foil. There might be enough to pay the price of his vengeance.

He pried at the golden edge with his dagger and pulled back a large sheet of the shining metal. Then he inspected the rest of the chamber for more opportunities and found several more deposits of the valuable gilding.

These must be enough to pay the price of the sword.

He kept them in a pouch at his belt. When the day came, the gold was just enough to pay for the expensive weapon. He felt relief knowing that he would be able to face the enemy.

One thing remained to do. On the next Saturday night, he took the blade with him to the tree. When the vision came of far-away places he saw within the light that he should take the blade and place it in the light.

He set the scabbard aside and lifted the blade to the light. As soon as it entered the radiance, the letters along the silver began to glow in a soft red light. They seemed to take on the power Giacomo wanted for them. They would have the power to fight the devil which he pursued.

He pondered whether to face the priest-devil at the church or to follow him until he showed his true nature. In the end, the later seemed a better choice.

He followed the priest every time he left the rectory, hoping to find an opportunity to confront him. It was several weeks before his chance came.

A fog had rolled into the city. Those that braved its chill could see only a few yards in front of them. Giacomo had a difficult time following, but once the priest turned into the street that led to the catacomb, he knew where he was going. Giacomo ran ahead to intercept him.

He waited at the grate which blocked entrance to the tunnels. It was only a few minutes before Father Andonito appeared in the mist. Again, he was leading his victim, which was a young man in tattered rags, to the place where he fed.

Something in Giacomo told him to wait, wait until he was at the sarcophagus.

Maybe once there he would have the chance he needed to face the devil.

He was also plagued by a sense of honor. He would not attack without warning. That was ungentlemanly. It would go against all he'd been taught by his mentor. If anything, this was a vengeance that should be done in complete honor. Even if there was no one else to see.

He slid in behind the monster and followed at a discreet distance. In the catacomb, there was no mist. The soft cold light which seemed to follow his adversary guided him along.

He'd decided to make his intention known before the devil had a chance to feast. Perhaps he could save the boy's life.

Once he reached the chamber, Giacomo boldly stepped from the shadows and said in a loud voice. "Devil. Step away and face me. I will have justice for the death of my master!" With that he drew his new blade and took the classic rapier stance. The point of his blade was slightly dipped and his hand was in a high guard turned to the left so that the blade was nearly parallel to the floor.

The priest turned and smiled. His features seemed demonic and twisted. The angle of his cheeks seemed higher than before. The sallow of his skin stretched. His teeth were bared and sharp like two dozen white nails jutting at random angles from its gums.

A red haze seemed to hang in the air. Giacomo felt a pain of fear raise up in his heart. He felt heavy and he seemed to lose control of his body. The terror he felt ran through him in waves. Suddenly he felt the desperate need to run.

But he could not move. He was trapped in the chamber with the devil. His life would end here because he stood by his own honor. If he would have attacked without warning, he might have ended it. Now his hopes where lost.

He'd spent a fortune on the blade he held immobile in his outstretched hand. The blade with writing he did not understand along its length. The words he could not fathom. The words that empowered the blade. The words that freed him of the enemy's power.

"You have done all this to kill me and yet it shall be you who dies," Andonito's twisted smile seemed to spread wider. He slowly approached. Each step seemed to increase the fear which now overwhelmed Giacomo.

The words on the blade were his only hope. What power they had must be able to free his mind from the unnatural fear which continued to build. What did they say? How could he have been so arrogant?

His mind began to jump between the blade and the fear. Each was related. Each fed off the other. His fear fed the blade. The blade devoured the fear.

At once he knew the truth. With all his mental reserve, Giacomo focused the fear on the letters of the blade. He could feel his control returning. He knew he would be able to defend himself now.

Andonito was now close enough for a long thrust from the tip of his blade. Giacomo waited. He wanted to be sure of his strike.

The priest reached forward to take Giacomo's sword.

At that moment, Giacomo chose to strike. He thrust the tip straight into his enemy's chest. Ten inches of blade buried into him just below the heart.

Surprise flashed across the evil face. Then quickly an even larger smile. He seemed to think he would be able to survive the encounter.

Giacomo twisted his wrist and dropped his hand, forcing the tip of the blade upward. Though his enemy tried to slip backward, he found the blade was stuck in his ribs.

It was then that the writing on the blade began to glow the same pale red it had when in the light of the tree. The devil began to thrash against the blade while Giacomo tried desperately to hold on to the grip.

With a sudden shudder the monster broke free, snapping the end of the blade off.

The force of the motion caused Giacomo to fall against the sarcophagus. He reached out to steady himself but the basket of the guard was smashed in the process. Giacomo's hand was trapped in the twisted wire and metal of the hilt.

He ignored his broken hand and watched as the creature sank to the floor of the chamber, writhing in pain.

Giacomo watched, waiting to make sure the thing would die.

It continued to struggle though and Giacomo decided to cut the head from its body. Nothing could survive such an injury. He was rewarded with silence.

The young man who had been standing aside while the encounter took place seemed to suddenly come to his senses. He ran from the chamber yelling of the murder of the priest.

Giacomo realized he would be blamed for an unjust death of Andonito. He fled through the tunnels and emerged just as a party of the city guard arrived. The boy pointed him out and in a loud voice proclaimed him the murderer of the priest.

Wanting to avoid compounding his trouble, he took to flight up one of the nearby side streets.

Giacomo was a man of action, in excellent health and vigor. Quickly he outpaced the pursuing guardsmen and escaped. He knew they'd search for him at the Belino estate.

In order to avoid bringing the family he loved into his problem, he fled to the docks where he quickly boarded a ship bound for Gibraltar. From there he decided to seek his fortune in the new world.

# New Methods

*3 years ago*

It seemed to the twins that their tactic had failed. Not only did the enemy manage to escape but they were left with several unanswered questions. What to do next was the most disturbing.

Up until then they'd managed to operate on a lose plan. They both figured Orochi would not repeat his mistake. They were relegated to reviewing every detail of his known past to try to find a way of cornering him again. This time they'd need to act quickly in to ensure that he would not escape.

They'd underestimated him. Worse yet, Jamas had done it twice. It didn't sit well with her that the creature had gotten the better of her.

For Kayle it was more of an academic problem. Though he was annoyed at having let the chance slip away, he also realized that the greater the challenge, the greater the victory. He'd always felt that way. He rarely let competition cause him distress. He viewed chasing Jamas' villain as just that.

After driving back to the city, they camped out at Kayle's apartment to go over all the clues.

The only consistent clue they had was that he tended to "hunt" the same way. It seemed the nightclub scene was his preferred hunting ground.  The question became, where would he go next?

The twins went over his corporate holdings and looked for any location they hadn't had contacts with him.  They were going on the idea that he would not return to any previous location, thinking that he would be vulnerable.

It was Jamas who decided to return to Tokyo, working on the theory that Orochi might feel the need to return home.  She'd reasoned that he had, over the course of his career, ventured out to other places but had some deep connection with his home.

He'd built an empire there.  His familiarity would let him feel safe.  She was sure now that he'd not come to San Francisco to escape her, but on a business trip to support his vast international holdings.

The city seemed to be alive any time of day or night.  People travelled by car and by foot in every corner.  Lights from thousands of advertising signs flashed inducement to the masses.  A person could easily hide in Tokyo.

A layer of clouds reflected the multicolored hue back down to the inhabitants, making the night seem like day.

Jamas and Kayle sat at a table in the back corner of the disco-tech.  It was dimmer in here than out in the street.  Loud music and strobing lights aided the spell of concealment that Jamas had prepared for the night of waiting.

They'd chosen this club due to its proximity to the headquarters of Orochi's business as well as for the fact that it seemed to be more heavily trafficked by him in the past. Finding information on deaths in the area was a matter of public record. Hours of pouring over the details gave them an indication that this might be his favorite haunt.

While they waited, they scanned the crowd looking for potential victims. It seemed a fruitless endeavor. If he didn't show, then there would be no victim. If he did show, then they would do their best to make sure there was no victim.

In reality there was nothing to do but wait and be patient.

Jamas felt her reserves of patience being drained more quickly as the night passed. Having Kayle here to temper her unease made the situation more palatable.

The random discussions in hushed tones she and he shared helped the time pass. She was grateful for the familiar company.

A number of studies have been done on the relationship that twins share. The one thing that they all seem to indicate is that twins, unlike the run of the mill siblings, seem to be calmer and more comfortable in each other's the presence. In addition, the same studies show that the reverse is also true. They seem to feel more anxious and less at ease when parted for any length of time. With Jamas and Kayle, the rule seemed to be exaggerated. Together they were a well-oiled machine.

So far the night was shaping up to be somewhat boring. They'd not seen their enemy yet and though there were still several hours till closing time, Jamas was getting itchy for action.

Kayle recognized the symptoms and offered conversation and planning as a way of alleviating her growing angst.

The one real advantage they had was that they knew Orochi was afraid of them. This indicated he could be stopped. The combination of Jamas and he had always been up to any task and both felt confident that they could deal with Orochi easily if they could simply cut off his retreat. It was for that reason they'd enlisted some help.

Stationed around the room were several agents of the Togogura family. Though notorious criminals in most respects, they did have the common goal of seeing the end of the creature. Their clan chief had instructed them to cut off any escape for the creature but to let the Drakson twins do the work of destroying it.

Honor would be served by allowing the clan to be part of the trap. The chance for success would be greater if the clan allowed Jamas and Kayle to do their work. Though Jamas suspected that they might renege and try to destroy it themselves, she still felt it was a better plan than to try to tackle the thing without their aid. And in the end, as long as it was killed, she would be satisfied.

The night continued to slowly pass without Orochi making an appearance. Kayle continued to scan the room hoping to see the familiar face of their adversary. Suddenly one of the patrons caught his attention. He didn't look like Orochi but there was a familiar glint in his eye that made him think that he'd seen him before.

He nudged Jamas and nodded in the direction of the man.

Jamas looked over and frowned. She shook her head for a moment then stopped and smiled. With a whisper she sent along a spell of seeing.

The familiar red glow surrounded the man instantly and his features transformed into those of the man they were chasing. Kayle raised his hand as if to wave the waitress to his table. This was a sign to the rest of the hunters that Orochi was in the house.

Still, they waited for him to make his move. He would be most vulnerable when using his powers to mesmerize someone. He would need to concentrate on them intently to bring that person under his control.

Orochi stood up and walked to a young Japanese man at the bar. Kayle smiled as it was one of the Togogura's. Perhaps this would be easier than they thought. No. They'd underestimated him before. Vigilance was called for now. Patience and vigilance.

Jamas showed signs of anticipation. She wrung her hands under the table to loosen the knuckles and hide the slight tremble. He eyes shifted from Orochi to each of the Togogura agents as though counting the odds of success.

For Kayle's part, he breathed in long slow breaths. He seemed calm and collected. Though he maintained a vigilant watch on the happenings all around, he seemed completely at ease.

A short conversation had commenced between Orochi and the Togogura agent. From where they sat, neither could hear what was said. It seemed to Jamas that something was amiss and she nodded in a way that indicated to Kayle she had reservations.

Their long close connection as twins had helped them develop an unspoken language of communication. A slight nod one way or the other indicated something important that only the other would understand.

Kayle trusted his sister's intuition and looked around, trying to reanalyze the situation. A nod from him indicated that he was now aware of the same misgiving.

Still, they were here and so was Orochi. This was their best chance to end his reign of terror. Kayle quickly waved his hand in a small motion to indicate they should wait and see what happens. Her response indicated she was ready for anything.

Orochi turned toward the twins and began walking toward them as though he could see through the spell she'd used to conceal them.

Once within speaking distance, he smiled and said "No worry, your spell is working perfectly. I cannot see who you are. The question you have is how do I know you are those two who have dogged my steps back and forth across the pacific? You see, nothing is as you think. Though my family has been hunting me for centuries, it was not for the reasons you have been told." An evil smirk creased his face.

"I am the instrument of their honor. Those long centuries ago, my master had me killed for the offences of another. As I committed the ritual seppuku, I swore that my spirit would not rest till my death was avenged. My family stood by me and maintained me with the flesh of the living till I was strong enough to recreate my body. Then as I assumed my rightful place at the side of the emperor, the new threat of western arrogance took apart the world of my ancestors so I again tried to rebuild my honor. This time in business. If I could not defeat the enemy in battle, I would rule them with finance. And now if you two would only step aside, I am close to my goal. But I know that you are both honorable warriors as well. So, you must die to finish your task and I will kill to keep the honor of my family."

"We should stop talking then and get on with the show!" Jamas jumped to her feet. The chair she sat upon spun back and crashed to the floor.

Kayle stood in concert with his sister. Though standing, neither took fighting stances. Both stood with arms relaxed and knees slightly bent.

The uninterested crowd seemed to realize that something dangerous was about to happen and began to rush for the doors.

Each of the Togogura agents began to wade toward the siblings.

Orochi began by generating fear. It was intense and powerful. Even with the spells that Jamas had woven, the twins felt blasted by the emotional attack.

Jamas spoke a word of magic and put up an invisible shield which deflected the majority of the terror and allowed them both to counter the attack.

Kayle stepped forward and punched Orochi in the chest. He attacked at a slight angle which allowed Jamas to move in from the other side.

As Orochi stumbled back from the attack, Jamas kicked in a quick arc to the opposite side of his face.

Orochi ducked quickly. Then he moved so fast that the twins could barely follow him. One strike to each chest knocked them back a step.

As he attacked, Orochi's face seemed to age. Lines crept along the natural creases and his cheeks and eyes seemed to sink. Whatever power he was using seemed to be draining him of his life force.

Jamas thought that if they could continue to keep him using his power, they might be able to drain him to the point of weakness. Perhaps then they could finish him.

By now the first of the Togogura agents had come close enough to be a threat. Another unspoken communication between the twins resolved them to use non-lethal techniques against the normal humans.

Kayle stepped away to defend his sister's back while she continued to harry Orochi.

The first agent that stepped forward was rewarded by a broken collar bone and a clean knockout punch. As he fell, the next stepped forward to challenge Kayle.

Jamas launched a series of brutal attacks at her antagonist. These forced him back against a table where he leaned backward to avoid the fury of her onslaught.

With a quick motion, he flipped over the table, rolling backward so fast that Jamas was taken off guard by the kick he launched. This caught her in the chin. As he landed, the lines on his face were deeper and more prominent. He seemed hunched and aged as he recovered.

Jamas rolled her head back to absorb as much of the kick as she could. The impact was still enough to crash her teeth together and cause a slight dizziness. She shook it off and quickly resumed her attack.

Kayle had dealt with four of the dozen Togogura's. Two more came forward simultaneously. As one jabbed a punch at his face, he intercepted it. He crossed his hands pulling the fist of the first across his body, creating a human shield against the second.

The second stepped back to avoid hitting his companion. Kayle then reversed the motion of his hand, flipping the first to the floor with a heavy crash. He lay still trying desperately to intake enough air.

Kayle quickly stepped over him and landed a kick on the knee of the next man. As he doubled over, Kalye ran his knee into the man's face, causing him to flip over backward and land with a crash.

Kayle found himself in the center of four more of the attackers.

Orochi drew up straight and tall. His arms hung at his side slightly away from his body.

Jamas felt as though he were preparing a spell. She whispered a protection and waited for the unknown effect of Orochi's spell.

The room began to shake. Orochi's hands were trembling in time with the quake he seemed to be generating. Objects fell from the tables and shelves. Occasionally one of these would fly toward Jamas. Glasses, broken bits of wood, and bottles of whatever drinks were served made up the majority of the flying weapons. The first struck her in the back. The second she deflected with a swipe of her hand. She dodged the third and fourth and fifth.

A whirlwind of glass and wood now spun in the air around a rapidly aging monster. It's hair had gone thin and white. Where there had been a youthful caste now the ravages of centuries were displayed.

The Togogura agents were trapped in the same tornado. They'd managed to hunker down behind an overturned table only after three of their comrades had been rendered out of action by the dervish.

Kayle drew his short sword and leaned into what felt like a storm. As objects closed in on him, he was able to deflect them, using quick flicks of his wrist. He felt as though he were fencing with the forces of nature. He tried to move close enough to aid his sister.

She had worked her way toward Orochi. Now within striking distance, she threw another series of brutal punches at his face. Each connected easily.

He seemed unaffected by the impacts and continued to shake and shiver as the room spun around.

Kayle stepped forward and slid the tip of his blade past his sister and into the creature's left side just below the ribs. With a twist, he sliced upward to its heart.

The room was suddenly silent and still. For several moments, the spinning objects hung suspended in the air. A loud sigh ushered from Orochi. Then he crumpled to the floor and disappeared in a cloud of dust. As the dust settled, a loud clamor of thousands of objects crashing into the floor broke the silence.

# Final Confrontation
*Now*

Nick and Conner peered over the slight rise.  A grassy field stood between them and the large estate which they knew now held the creature they intended to kill.

That they still used the word kill was only an ingrained military metaphor.  Their enemy had been dead for centuries.  After much research and a foray to England, it was discovered that the one they sought had been one of the first creatures created by the monster that Kayle and Jamas had destroyed years before.

The flight to Africa had been used to discuss tactics. The first class cabin seemed an ill secured location from which to contemplate what would undoubtedly be a violent conflict. They kept their voices low and did their best to avoid anyone overhearing their planning session.

They brought no weapons other than a short sword and a military style knife.  The sword had belonged to Chris. Nick had been informed that it had been Maria's brothers before it was given to Chris.  There would be plenty of weapons available for them to use once they made their move.

The hidden journal which sat on one of Jamas' shelves had told the story of how they'd been duped by the Japanese clan and nearly killed themselves.  Only vigilance and quick thinking had saved them.

Now the two companions waited for the moment to strike. Maria slid up next to Conner and kissed him on the cheek. Her smile betrayed the depth of love she felt for him.

Nick felt a twinge of jealousy. To know that his friends had found happiness softened the blow that Nick had been feeling lately. His own loneliness.

Nick had never had a real romantic relationship. There were a few abortive attempts but each ended the same way. He was not the settling down kind of man. It had taken him a long time to realize that his deep friendship with Conner was because Conner had been like him. When the two minds that had been Conner and Keith had merged, he was no longer a kindred soul. That was the tinge he felt now. A deeper loneliness. One that told him he was alone and unique.

In a way, he felt strengthened by the feeling. He could do what he had to do. He needn't fear the pain that might be inflicted should he die in his work. He need not worry about a loved one at home worrying over him while he was away.

Instead he could concentrate on whatever needed to be done. Even morality could be bent a little knowing that no one who he loved would question his character. He would never disappoint. He would simply do the thing.

Maria informed the two that the creature must be in the house. Her spells of detection had been much more refined than the one her sister created. Maria had developed a new formula which was much more specific. She could also lend the vision to her companions for a short time. She'd wait till they entered the estate first as the spell would only be active for less than ten minutes.

The sun slowly sank below the horizon as they waited patiently. They'd decided to make their move just after the sun went down.

In the fading light, they could move quickly and still have complete confidence in their own sight. The disadvantage was, they'd be visible to the enemy till the twilight completely faded. Here on the plain of Africa, the evening was short. The time between sunset and darkness was counted in minutes.

Nick rechecked the area based on his earlier visit. The guards had been increased but the basic movement and location remained the same. People were creatures of habit and the mundane act of standing guard seemed to express those habits in an unhindered way. If you add more men, they will still follow the practices of the one there first unless specifically directed otherwise.

These men were not the highly disciplined kind. They were rather lazy at approaching their duties. It didn't mean they weren't dangerous. It only caused Nick to wonder if there was anything he hadn't taken into account.

The sun had fully set. The three interlopers stalked quickly and quietly toward the estate. As they moved, Conner and Nick scanned the ground for tripwires and traps while advancing. Nick stopped the team as he discovered a section of tripwires. These were connected to a series of improvised claymore mines. A charge of plastic explosive and ball bearings was attached to a metal back-plate. The detonator was a simple blasting cap. Nick disarmed the system and confirmed that the team could move on.

The stop had taken several minutes and by then it was near complete darkness. The stars would be the only light as they'd chosen a night without the moon for their incursion.

The team stopped at the edge of the clearing in which the large house stood. Maria used her spell on Nick and Conner. Nick also checked the entire area for changes in what he'd observed.

The guards still followed the same paths. Though there would only be a ten second split between each group of two instead of the twenty he'd enjoyed on his earlier visit.

He informed the others then quickly ran across to the low wall which surrounded the estate. The next pair of guards came around the corner just as he settled into the shadow of the wall.

Conner was moving his hand up and down to an unseen timer. He counted in tens then stopped for the one count. Then started again at two. Pause. Two. Three. Four. Five. Six. Seven, eight, nine. Ten. "Go," he whispered.

Maria ran across and settled next to Nick.

The next one count and Conner joined his Friends.

As they crouched in the darkness, Nick continued to tap the air with his hand informing the team of the timing they would need.

At five, two guards would pass just above where they were. Nick and Conner would attack in synchronicity.

Three. Four. Five.

The two men stood quickly and hopped over the wall. Both guards were startled by the sudden manifestation of danger. Both were dead before seven. The knives of the two veterans silently robbed them of life.

On nine, the bodies were tossed over the wall, their firearms now in the hands of Nick and Conner. At ten, the three quickly crossed to the side door at the garage.

They ignored the camera above knowing they had perhaps a minute before they would be discovered and guards sent to intercept them.  Now at close proximity to the target, speed had replaced caution as the primary concern.  Nick kicked the door open and leveled his weapon inside.  He saw no resistance and moved in quickly, scanning through his sight picture for any potential threat.

Conner followed quickly moving to cover the left while Nick shifted to the right.

Maria entered behind them.

The garage was empty.  There were no cars or people in the great bay which seemed larger by the absence.  Nick leveled his hand and shot it toward the door leading into the house.  Both men felt that the area was a perfect killing ground.  No cover for them to use.

They crossed quickly to the door and ripped it open.  This time Conner slipped in first followed by Maria.  Nick gazed behind the group making sure they were not in jeopardy from behind.

The hallway led to the kitchen.  The kitchen opened into the dining area which in turn led to the central foyer.  At each door, the group looked for signs of the creature they were here to kill.  It seemed to be above them in a room they had yet to discover.

When asked later, Nick described what he saw as a sort of red ghost floating in space at a distance.  Even though he could not see everything around him in complete clarity he could make out a figure that seemed to be sitting in a chair. It moved as though it was writing at a desk. The figure was a whiff of red mist.The group moved across the foyer to a large staircase which wrapped the arced side of the semicircular room. A shot from above indicated they'd been discovered.

Conner leveled his stolen Uzi in the direction of the shot and let a burst fly.

Nick couldn't see past either Maria or Conner but he could tell Conner had hit his target. The familiar thump of a body falling from maybe fifteen feet onto the floor to his right was all the evidence he needed.

Nick maintained his rearward vigil. A man quickly stuck his head around the corner below. Nick replied with a burst, from his own weapon. This he directed at the corner of the wall behind which his opponent had ducked. He was rewarded when he saw the man fall into sight from behind his supposed cover. The drywall and wood studs were ill suited to stopping the nine millimeter rounds which easily tore through.

They'd managed the landing and crossed in the direction of the red apparition. There was a short hallway which offered doors to both sides. The ones on the right were positioned between the three and the creature.

At the door, Nick positioned himself to the right while Conner stood to the left. The handle of the door was on Nick's side. Conner brought up his weapon and readied himself.

Nick checked the handle to see if it was locked. It was not. Then he nodded to Conner and twisted it open. Conner stepped in and fired two bursts. Nick followed rapidly, moving to cover the opposite side of the room. There was a wall between them and the figure.

The figure was now standing. It moved across the room toward the hallway.

Maria watched as the figure came closer. She was still in the hall. Setting herself up for the potential confrontation was only a matter of changing her stance and bringing her arms up in an arc level with her waist.

The door opened and out stepped an ancient looking man. He turned toward Maria and his eyes narrowed.

The pain and terror of fear ripped through her. She'd felt the effect before and thought she could stand it but was so amazed at how strong it was when coming from this very powerful wight.

She could not bring herself to say the word to activate the spell meant to release her from the paralyzing effect of his gaze.

Nick stepped back out of the room and leveled his weapon. Though he also felt the same fear that she did, his years of living in its company allowed him some relief. He was able to pull the trigger and send a burst at the creature.

The wight waved his hand and the bullets dissolved into dust before impact. The action distracted him enough for Maria to use her spell.

Though the fear diminished, it was still a stinging reminder that they faced a powerful opponent.

The creature strode forward and reached out with its hands, attempting to grapple with Maria.

She stepped back, allowing Nick freedom to fire indiscriminately. The creature again transformed the rounds, making them useless.

Maria moved forward to engage it in hand fighting. She knew that she needed to avoid its grasping claws and its bite. A kick landed against it, pushing it back a step.

It was then that she reached back and said in a loud voice, "Sword."

Nick slipped it from the sheath at his hip and leaned forward to offer it to her, handle first.

Reaching for the weapon, she moved like a lioness as she danced around an ungraceful attack from the enemy.

She gripped the rapier by its jeweled handle and settled into a classic fencing pose.

The creature grimaced in hatred as she presented the blade.

"That silver has killed two of my kin. It is time I took it out of the game," he said as he reached forward so quickly that Maria was unable to defend herself.

He gripped the sword just behind the cross guard and pulled it from her grasp. With a quick spin, he pivoted on a heel and thrusted the tip at Maria's face. She managed to slide sideways just in time to avoid the deadly attack.

As the creature drew back to ready itself for another attack, she jabbed her hand out and gripped it behind the wrist.

Maria uttered a single word of classic French "Punition!" which caused a bolt of pain to rack the creature hard enough for it to drop the sword.

Nick stepped forward and caught the falling blade midair. In one motion, he leaned in close and drove the blade upward. The tip entered the creature just below the sternum and penetrated all the way through the left collar.

The thing convulsed several times as its now ashen features seemed to crack and flake away.

Conner stepped into view just in time to watch as the creature slowly dissolved to dust.

"It's over." Maria sighed.

"For now. There will always be another battle. There will always be evil in the world." Conner replied.

"We'll be here." Nick added.

"Yes." Marias voice was quiet and reserved.

They'd seen enough over the last few years to know that they would be needed again. The unasked questions remained. When?

They left the compound the same way they'd entered. There was no resistance. It felt strangely peaceful. Nick seemed to be morose and silent. As was his habit, he'd spend hours reflecting after a fight.

Once free of the compound they climbed into the car they'd left waiting several miles from the estate.

On the drive back to civilization, each pondered the meaning of their new life. The Team seemed to have a new chance to aid humanity. Perhaps this was the first step in that struggle.

Maybe the mission had never changed. The enemy might be different but there would always be creatures like these to keep at bay. Like everyone, having a purpose gives meaning to their life. It was not a start or even a change, simply another stop on the road they'd been travelling.

# Epilogue

*3 years ago*

The tall Georgian church was considered a classic example of the type. Four tall columns flanked the double entry and the clapboard siding had been whitewashed to an even, flat tone. Along the columns and surrounding the double door were lines of characters from dozens of languages.

The inside had been decorated in the style of the times. A row of long walnut benches ran down either side. Stained glass windows along the side walls depicted a variety of scenes from the gospels. At the bottom of each pane there could be seen additional text and obscure writings which seemed out of place in the seemingly traditional place of worship.

The back wall behind the alter had been constructed to represent something atypical of a church from the early eighteenth century. The glass radiated a depiction of the settlers in the area meeting and becoming friendly with the natives who lived in the place before them.

The alter itself was a study of contradiction. Though the podium and benches behind might be seen in any church, the ever-present symbols stood out on every surface. these might have been considered cultish to other churches. Here, in relationship to the rest of the church, they seemed to belong.

The puritanical Calvinists who'd build the church had been culturally altered by interaction with the local Manandan tribe. It showed in the somewhat expressive art with which the entire hall had been decorated.

Near the altar, several metal chairs had been set up. These faced the first row of pews. Two men and a woman occupied them. On the facing pew sat two women and a man.

They were all dressed in a somewhat traditional style of clothing which on first look, might indicate they were in mourning. The black slacks and skirts were mostly conservatively cut. The jackets covered white blouses and shirts. Along the seams of every garment, lines of writing in ancient languages formed interesting patterns.

To someone who didn't know them, they might seem to be Quakers. Though not far from the truth, they were in point of fact six siblings who were troubled by recent events.

The youngest of the group was Maria. She was several months pregnant and had obviously been crying. The red around her eyes and streaks of mussed eyeliner indicated she held some recent sorrow.

Two others seemed anxious to tell a story of some import. They'd recently returned from Asia with a tale of a new threat which the family might need to investigate. Though they had yet to inform the family of their adventures, a very real concern was displayed by the twins. Jamas was the older by only moments. Tall and athletic, her dark features indicated a heritage which included the Manandans. She was the only of the siblings to express her genetics in such a way.

Her brother Kayle was only slightly taller. His heavy frame indicated a highly toned and developed musculature beneath the black and white he wore.

The tallest of the group seemed lanky by comparison. His pants were just a little too short and his entire wrist could be seen extending from the sleeves of what seemed to be an ill cut jacket.

He had been involved in a lengthy research project which had ended with the disappearance of their father. The event for which they had gathered.

The oldest brother sat nearest the alter. His paternal demeanor offered a great deal of calm during the upsetting time. He hadn't informed the others that he too had recently been involved in an extension of the family vocation.

As a doctor of note, he'd attended a conference upstate and ran into some rather unsavory characters. They had belonged to a cult which wanted to bring about the end of the world by summoning a creature of power from the dark realm. The fact that Thomas had thwarted their plan, and that they had no real clue as to the nature of the dark realm from which they'd planned to summon the daemon made it something of a comedy of errors on their part.

Stevanie was the other medical doctor in the family. She seemed to be mindful of the rest in the way a mother might be. Her soft sad eyes looked upon each with a grace and dignity which she genuinely felt. Of all the siblings, she was the most emotional. Though she hid her feelings well lest it worried the others.

As they talked and reminisced, they each knew that things would be different from that point on. Knowing that their father had probably been killed in his recent experiment was only the start of some new challenge that they must face. Each of the siblings were beset by both disbelief and sadness. But within all of that they knew that they must endure for they had work to do. With the rift now seeming to challenge their control, they would need to act quickly.

None had a plan as yet. Things had happened so fast. A quick decision was taken to wander to the diner and have a meal before the long discussion would begin.

They filed out of the diner and walked slowly toward the metal and glass restaurant. As regulars, the staff, which were also their relatives, would know what they wanted and be amiable about their quiet remorse.

As they got closer, Zach realized that someone was already seated near the front.

Zach's hand quickly gripped the pendant which hung beneath his shirt. A soft warm sensation flowed from the gem within the golden hoop and into his hand generating a feeling of hope and calmness.

"We should talk to that man," he said softly. "He might be the answer."